Elfangor's Secret

Look for other ANIMORPHS® titles by K.A. Applegate:

#1 *The Invasion*
#2 *The Visitor*
#3 *The Encounter*
#4 *The Message*
#5 *The Predator*
#6 *The Capture*
#7 *The Stranger*
#8 *The Alien*
#9 *The Secret*
#10 *The Android*
#11 *The Forgotten*
#12 *The Reaction*
#13 *The Change*
#14 *The Unknown*
#15 *The Escape*
#16 *The Warning*
#17 *The Underground*
#18 *The Decision*
#19 *The Departure*
#20 *The Discovery*
#21 *The Threat*
#22 *The Solution*
#23 *The Pretender*
#24 *The Suspicion*
#25 *The Extreme*
#26 *The Attack*
#27 *The Exposed*
#28 *The Experiment*
#29 *The Sickness*

<MEGAMORPHS>

#1 *The Andalite's Gift*
#2 *In the Time of Dinosaurs*
#3 *Elfangor's Secret*

The Hork-Bajir Chronicles

ALTERNAMORPHS

The First Journey

Elfangor's Secret

K.A. Applegate

SCHOLASTIC INC.
New York Toronto London Auckland Sydney
Mexico City New Delhi Hong Kong

Cover illustration by David B. Mattingly

ISBN 0-590-03639-4

12 11 10 9 8 7 6 5 4 3 2 1 9/9 0 1 2 3 4/0

Printed in the U.S.A. 40

First Scholastic printing, May 1999

For Michael and Jake

Elfangor's Secret

Prologue

Aristh Elfangor-Sirinial-Shamtul was done with war. Sick to death of it.

He had caused the Yeerk infestation of his own prince and created the abomination now called Visser Three. He had been unable to save his friend and fellow *aristh* Arbron, now trapped forever in the body of a Taxxon.

Disaster piled on disaster. Failure on failure.

Now he was done with it all. He had escaped to the planet called Earth along with Loren, the human he loved. He would morph to human. Live as a human. Get lost amid the humans. Maybe even somehow, someway, find happiness.

But he still had possession of the greatest

weapon the galaxy had ever known: the Time Matrix.

The Time Matrix could travel backward through time the way a Z-space craft could travel through space. It gave the person who controlled it power beyond imagining. A person traveling backward could rewrite history.

Using the Time Matrix, entire species could be exterminated. More than exterminated: They could be made never to have existed.

It was too much power to trust to anyone. *Especially*, Elfangor thought bitterly, *a failure like him.*

The Time Matrix was a sphere, taller than a human. Destroying it was physically impossible. But it could be hidden. For a while, at least.

He found an empty place. Nothing but trees. Using only the equipment available to any human, he dug a hole and rolled the device into it. He covered it.

And then, he morphed to human.

Two hours later, he was no longer an Andalite. He was trapped. Human. Human forever, no longer a part of the vast war raging between Andalite and Yeerk. He was free.

Or so he thought.

Many years later, he returned to the same spot. Desperate enough to try to use the Time

Matrix. The spot had become a construction site. This time, there would be no escape.

His time ran out. Just a few yards from the machine that could have given him all the time in the world.

CHAPTER 1
Tobias

My name is Tobias.

In the history of Earth I may be the strangest creature ever to live. I mean it. You have to look at mythology to find anything as weird as I am. Maybe the griffin, which was supposed to be half lion and half eagle, or the centaur, half human and half horse, or whatever.

But those are myths. I am reality.

I am half human, half hawk. Red-tailed hawk, actually. *Buteo jamaicensis*, like that tells you much.

Homo sapiens, meet *Buteo jamaicensis*.

But that's not even the end of the story. Because in addition to that bizarreness, there's this:

My father was an Andalite who had morphed to human.

So you could say I'm *Homo sapiens*, *Buteo jamaicensis*, and Andalite. What would the Latin name be for Andalites? Don't know.

Is the glass half empty or half full? That's what they always ask, to see if you're an optimist or a pessimist. Am I some kind of hideous freak of nature, a twisted concoction of mismatched parts? Or am I something new and wonderful?

Depends on the day. Depends on whether I'm with Melissa, wanting to make her happy, wanting her to hold my hand, wanting to be able to take her to a movie and a burger afterward like any other guy can do with a date, maybe even hold her hand, maybe kiss her, maybe . . . Yeah, at times like that, the glass is half empty.

But there are other times. Times when the sun is high and hot. When the cumulus clouds are like gigantic mountains floating through a blue sky. Times when the warm air billows up beneath my wings and I barely have to flap and all of a sudden I'm so high, so totally, absolutely free, free in a way I never was as a human, free to soar and soar, alone, nothing but the sound of the wind ruffling across my feathers . . . and on those days the glass is spilling over.

This was a full-glass day.

I was high in the air, I don't know, maybe a thousand feet up, the beach just ahead of me, a sweet thermal lifting me up. I could see the ocean, I could see the beach and all the people spread out there.

On a day like this, it was hard to be a pessimist. Yeah, Earth was being invaded by the Yeerks. Yeah, all that stood against them were five kids and one Andalite with the useful power to absorb the essence — what Ax calls "DNA" — of animals and then morph into them.

And yes, we were probably even losing the last war that humanity might ever fight as a free species. But on a stunning day like this, what I saw spread out below me was not possible Controllers, but people having a nice day at the beach, loving the sun, loving the warmth, taking it easy.

Even the slaves, standing by to attend to their masters and mistresses, seemed to be having a good time.

CHAPTER 2
Jake

Tobias came swooping in through the open hayloft.

<It's clear,> he reported.

I gave him a slight nod of the head. But I didn't acknowledge his presence beyond that. Cassie's slave girl was still in the room, cleaning out the cage of an injured and very vocal goose. And as Cassie is always reminding us, the fact that a slave may not be as bright as a regular person does not mean they can't tell tales.

This particular slave was mostly deaf, which of course partly accounted for her status. But Cassie claimed the girl was otherwise reasonably smart.

Cassie grabbed the girl's arm to get her attention, then, enunciating very clearly, said, "You can go now, September Twelve."

"Yes, mistress," the girl mumbled in her guttural, barely understandable speech. It came out "Yeth, mithreth." She turned and left the room.

Melissa looked up at Tobias and winked. "Been out flying?"

<You know it. The way the weather has been lately? I wouldn't miss a day like this.>

Ax arrived a moment later. Marco was with him.

"So, what's up?" Marco demanded. "What's this meeting about? Don't you realize I have important stuff going on? I lead a busy, busy life."

"Really?" Melissa asked naively. Melissa has never really gotten Marco's sense of humor.

<Marco, are you hanging out with your imaginary friends again?> Tobias asked.

"Excuse me, but I no longer need friends, real or imagined. I was playing Pong. My dad bought one for us. It's so cool. Even my mom was into it, which, in a way is sad, because seriously, who wants to be doing stuff with their mom?"

<Be nice to your mom,> Tobias said. <She'll probably end up being your prom date someday.>

Everyone laughed. Except Ax, of course, who had no idea what a prom was. Or why it would be funny to have your mom as a date.

He's not one of us. So what can you expect?

"We have information from the Chee," I said.

That made Marco groan. "Swell. Trouble. It always is. You know, Erek never contacts us to say, 'Hey let's have fun!' It's always 'Hey, how would you all like to go and get yourselves killed?' "

"What does Erek have?" Melissa asked.

"He has information that the Yeerks are putting together a new front organization. This one, unlike The Sharing, is aimed at a very specific target."

<What target?> Ax asked.

"Our troops," I said. "Especially troops being sent to the war in Brazil."

Cassie made a skeptical face. "Why would the Yeerks want to make Controllers of troops heading toward the jungle? What do they care whether we wipe out a bunch of Primitives?"

"It's not the war they care about," I said. "It's that things are tough for our boys down there, and I guess harsh conditions like that make it easy to get recruits. I mean, you're in the jungle, right? You figure 'How much worse could life get?' But most of the troops survive the war, they come back home, and the Empire rewards them with homesteads, slaves, cars, and so on. Lots of times they get jobs in government or else stay in the army. Suddenly the Yeerks have another one of their own in a position of power."

"What are we supposed to do about it?" Melissa asked. "That's thousands of miles away."

I shrugged. "I don't know. But what are we supposed to do, sit around while the Yeerks destroy the war effort? Let the jungle rats continue to take up valuable land that we need?"

"Yeah, it would be a pity if some of the Primitives escaped alive," Cassie said.

I shot a look at her. Had that been sarcasm?

She smiled blandly.

I had long suspected that Cassie might have slightly radical tendencies. A lot of blacks did. Blacks and a lot of Jews, although not in my family. My dad was a certified POE — Patriot of Empire.

Still, if you had any Jewish blood in you at all, you had to be extra careful so no one thought you were a radical.

I knew Cassie was soft-hearted toward her own slaves. But I'd never heard her make any kind of subversive remarks about the war. I'd always just assumed she was sentimental.

Even now, it was impossible to be sure what her tone of voice meant. I'm not very good at that kind of thing. I'm a mostly straightforward kind of guy. It might have been an innocent remark. Or not.

I felt my stomach churn. We couldn't denounce Cassie as a subversive. We knew for a fact that the Triple S was heavily infiltrated by Yeerks. Denounce her to the Triple S and we might as well just turn her over to the Yeerks, and then all was lost.

What was I supposed to do?

I intercepted Marco's gaze. He gave a slight nod. A "told you so" nod.

The question was, where would Melissa stand if it came down to eliminating Cassie? I knew Melissa was no radical. But she was Cassie's best friend, despite being white.

I shook my head, trying to focus. The Yeerks. *They* were my problem. Not radicals. If the human race survived the Yeerks we'd have all the time in the world to round up the radicals and take care of them.

In the meantime . . .

I gave Cassie a blank look, not acknowledging what she might have meant. "We have to try to deal with this. Personally, I don't want a world filled with Primitives any more than I want a world filled with Yeerks."

"Jungle rats and slugs," Marco said with a laugh. "Now there's a nice world for decent people to live in."

"Wonderful! Wonderful, I *love* it!"

The voice was unknown. I spun around, ready to do battle.

Standing there, as though it had appeared

from thin air, stood a creature who could not possibly be from Earth.

It looked at first glance like the mating of a small dinosaur and a large prune. It had two legs and balanced its body with a stubby tail.

The hands were weak, flimsy things, with too many joints.

The head didn't fit with the birdlike body. It was humanoid in shape, with a narrow lower jaw and big, mocking eyes.

The skin was wrinkled, like a prune. The flesh was dark, almost jet-black, relieved only by green that rimmed the eyes and mouth.

"Who are you?" I snapped.

"Me? Oh, I'm hurt. Devastated! You don't remember your old friend the Drode?"

CHAPTER 3
Jake

"I've never seen you before in my life," I said.

"Well . . . No. Not in *this* life, perhaps."

"Yeerk," Melissa said. "Some new host body."

"Marco," I said. He nodded. He began to slowly morph to grizzly bear, his favorite morph.

<Who are you?> Ax demanded. <Or should I say, *what*?>

The creature grinned. "You, at least, are no different, Aximili-Esgarouth-Isthill. Still the arrogant Andalite."

"Shut up, Ax," I snapped. "I am Supreme Leader here. I'll ask the questions." Having put one pushy alien in his place, I moved back to the other. “What do you want?” I demanded. Out of the corner of my eye I saw Marco changing.

The creature sighed. “Well, as much fun as it is to see you all this way, I suppose for us to move on I'll have to return you, temporarily at least, to your usual condition: sanctimonious, self-righteous, and utterly tedious.”

There was no flash of light. No bang. Nothing changed. Except that everything changed.

I changed.

Suddenly, instantly, I was a different person.

I stared at the Drode. I knew now who he was. *What* he was.

Whom he served.

I shot a look at Cassie. Then at the girl standing beside her. Melissa was gone. Rachel was there.

“So glad you're back with us, Rachel,” the Drode leered. “You know you're still my favorite Animorph.”

“What was all that?” Marco demanded mid-morph. “Some kind of hallucination?”

“No, no, no!” the Drode said. “It is glorious reality. Big Jake, Jake the perfect leader, Jake the compassionate, nothing more than a jumped-up little dictator with delusions of grandeur who insists on being called Supreme Leader!”

“No, that was not reality,” Cassie snapped. “I

do not own a slave! That's sickening! What are you talking about?"

"And where was I?" Rachel demanded.

"I was thinking how I'd have to turn Cassie in for not approving of some war down in Brazil," I admitted. "That's not reality."

"I will tell you about reality," the Drode said eagerly. "Your country is an empire, ruled by terror and torture. It has made war on the nations to the south. It slaughters peoples it calls 'Primitives.' It enslaves anyone with an IQ below eighty, as well as anyone born with what you call defects. All in all, it's my kind of place."

"That's bull!" Marco said hotly.

"I assure you it is all true. The Yeerks are within months of consolidating control. The lack of freedom among humans has made their conquest ever so much easier. Your few books, your two radio stations, your single television channel are all censored. Your technology is fifty years behind where it should be. Poverty is widespread, curable diseases run rampant, some women are forced to breed to repopulate the dominant white race while at the same time, in the major cities the poor and homeless are rounded up and shot —"

"Jake, let me take care of this little worm," Rachel said.

“What’s this all about, Drode?” I asked. I wasn’t at all sure I wouldn’t take Rachel up on her offer.

“The Time Matrix,” the Drode said.

<What?> Ax’s stalk eyes snapped around to stare. <That’s a myth! No such device ever existed.>

“Oh, it existed,” the Drode said. “It *exists*. It was found by a lowly human-Controller, who uses the name John Berryman. He’s an actor. Not a very successful one. A lowly Controller whose Yeerk was, until he lost the battle for Leera, none other than Visser Four. And why did he lose the battle for Leera? Why, because of all of you. Ironic, eh?”

“What does this have to do with all that other stuff?”

“The Yeerk, the former Visser Four, has used the Time Matrix. He has traveled backward in time and is changing historical events. He’s rewritten the past in an effort to bring about a Yeerk victory and give himself greater power. You . . . the other yous . . . are unaware that life was ever any different. You have all been raised in an environment of delightfully ferocious oppression. It’s all quite wonderful!”

“But slavery? Some genocidal war?” Cassie said, her voice cracking.

"Why are you here?" Rachel demanded.

The Drode sighed. "Sadly, I am here to offer you the chance to undo it all." He spread his hands wide and smiled a hideous smile. "I want to help."

CHAPTER 4

Cassie

I laughed. “You want to help. You. Meaning Crayak.”

“Yes, it is rather puzzling, isn’t it?” the Drode mocked.

<Why would you help?> Ax asked.

“It’s all part of a deal. My master, the great and glorious Crayak, and your friend, the simpering, meddling nitwit called the Ellimist, have a deal. Neither of them really approves of a mere Yeerk possessing the most powerful device in galactic history.”

“In other words, this Time Matrix could endanger Crayak himself,” Marco translated.

The Drode laughed. “Don’t be a fool. Nothing threatens great Crayak. However . . . one doesn’t want mere baboons blundering about with Time Matrices, does one? Who knows what harm they might do? Oh, sure, it's all fun and games when they end up starting genocidal wars or engendering race hatred —"

"Yeah, what's more fun than that?" Rachel said dryly.

"— but who knows what other damage a fool with such power may do?"

"Crayak could grab the Time Matrix himself," Jake said. "He has the power."

"Mmmm, well . . ." the Drode said.

Crayak and the Ellimist were to humans what humans are to ants. Nearly omnipotent creatures. One evil. One good.

Perhaps. We could never be entirely sure.

<The Rules,> Tobias said. <That's the problem. The rules of the game between Crayak and the Ellimist. Neither trusts the other with the Time Matrix. They don't need it themselves, but they might give it to their allies.>

The Drode put his hand to his ear. "Did I just hear a bird chirping?"

"You mentioned a deal," Marco said.

"Yes," the Drode said. "A deal. And here it is: The six of you will be allowed to follow the Time Matrix. The former Visser Four set off on his journey two days ago. You will be translated back to that point and then the quanta that make up your atoms will be . . . tuned. Yes, that's a good word for simple minds to comprehend. You'll be fine-tuned at the subatomic level to resonate with the movements of the Time Matrix as it travels through time. Your own memories and personalities will, of course, be buffered. Protected against changes."

<Resulting in what effect?> Ax demanded.

"Resulting in the effect that, like an echo, you will follow the Time Matrix. It plucks the chords of time and you reverberate." He stopped and shook his head in admiration of his own words. "Brilliantly explained, eh?"

"That's the deal?" Jake asked. "That's it?"

"There's something else, isn't there?" I asked the Drode.

The Drode laughed. "Oh, yes. There is something else, little Cassie. Cassie the killer with a conscience. Kill 'em, then cry over 'em. That's our Cassie."

"What's the something else?" I repeated, not letting the evil little creep see that his words had hit home.

"My master Crayak has demanded a price. A payment."

"A payment."

"Uh-huh," the Drode said in a parody of coyness.

"What?"

"One of you," the Drode said. "You can attempt to save your reality, put everything back where it belongs, end slavery, replace tyranny with democracy, millions of lives saved, let freedom ring, glory hallelujah in exchange . . . in exchange for one, single life."

"A life?" I asked.

"The life of one of you. That is my master Crayak's price: One of you must die."

CHAPTER 5
Cassie

"This is insane!" Marco said. "I mean, I've said things were insane before, but this is totally, abjectly insane!" He pointed at the Drode. "You go back and tell that manure pile Crayak, and the Ellimist, too: This isn't on us. They can fix this and leave us out."

"If we do nothing we go back to that other reality, don't we?" I said to the Drode. "Jake's some kind of junior Nazi, I'm a slave owner, all of us living like that?"

"Why wasn't I even in the group?" Rachel demanded.

"You? A violence-prone sociopath like you, Rachel?" the Drode said with a happy laugh. "You were in a reeducation camp. This world has little room for bold, aggressive females. You were being taught your place."

"Say what? My *what*?"

Suddenly, around the Drode's wrist, an oversized watch appeared. "You all have to decide," the Drode said, holding up the watch. "Two minutes. Ticktock, ticktock. Then all goes back to what it should be. Tick. Tock."

He was gone as suddenly as he had appeared.

"My *place*?" Rachel muttered, not quite believing the word. "No one teaches me my *place*."

"Okay. Two minutes. Visser Four is running around the past messing up the future. I don't think there's much question that we have to do this," Jake said.

<Prince Jake,> Ax said, <Have you forgotten that there will be a price to be paid? The life of one of us?>

Jake nodded. "No choice. Too much hangs on this. Millions of lives versus one? Not even a question."

"Bull," Marco said. "This isn't our fight. We sit this one out."

Rachel rounded on him. "What? And I go back to some reeducation camp? And slavery is back? And we're murdering natives down in the jungle or whatever? I don't think so. I can't believe even *you* could be this much of a weasel!"

But Rachel was wrong. It hadn't dawned on her yet, or maybe on the others. But I know Jake. There was only one life that Jake would trade away like this. Marco, too, knows Jake very well.

There was a history between Jake and the evil force called Crayak. It was Jake, more than any of us, who destroyed the Howlers and saved the Iskoort, two terrible blows against Crayak.

Jake assumed that he would be the one to die. Marco had seen this instantly. He wasn't arguing in favor of the awful future we'd seen. He was arguing for the life of his best friend.

"We're just going to let it all happen?" Rachel went on, in full outrage mode. "All we just experienced? Slavery? Censorship? Wars? Secret police rounding up the homeless and —"

"— and Pong?" Marco interrupted, breaking her momentum. "Look, don't be stupid. This could just be an elaborate trap. Anyway, how do we exactly fix the past? I mean, *exactly*? Does one of you have a history book stored away in his head? How do we fix history if we don't even know how it's broke?"

It was Ax who answered. <Whatever Visser Four is attempting to do, we undo.>

"Hey, it isn't that simple. Where do you think Visser Four is going to go to change history? He's going to wars, I guarantee you. Killing and dying.

And how do we know it isn't our own actions in the past that caused all this?"

<Time travel,> Tobias muttered. <Too much to get a human brain around. Too complex. Too many possibilities.>

"Okay, look, time is short. It's down to a vote," Jake said.

"What? The 'Supreme Leader' wants a vote?" Marco mocked. He was stalling. Eating up the two minutes.

<As bad a feeling as I get about this, I don't see how we can just blow this off,> Tobias said reluctantly.

"I'd rather die than be a slave owner," I said. "But . . ." I let it hang. I couldn't look at Jake. I felt sick.

I felt Marco staring at me. He wanted to see if I understood. I met his gaze. I nodded slowly.

I wanted to explain. Jake meant more to me than anyone in the world. He meant as much to me as my own parents. But I couldn't walk away from this. The society we'd just glimpsed? No. Whatever the price we paid we had to stop that.

Marco smiled a small, sad half smile, accepting my verdict.

<I will go where Prince Jake leads,> Ax said. <Also, I would very much like to see the Time Matrix.>

"Someone's going to teach me my place? Yeah, right. Let's do it," Rachel said, laughing at her own swagger.

"Marco?" Jake asked.

"Here's my vote: We go home and watch TV. Fifty channels, there's gotta be something on."

Jake shook his head. "I don't think so. The Drode said there was only one channel in that reality."

"One?" Marco asked, sounding shaken.

"One."

"Well, then Visser Four is my meat."

"Unanimous," Jake said, smiling in amusement at Marco.

Marco turned away from Jake. The grin disappeared. He looked like he wanted to cry.

Our eyes met again. And not for the first time I realized how smart Marco is underneath all the jokes. He knew we were going to do it. He knew his best friend's life might be the price we paid. He also knew we couldn't go into this hopeless battle thinking about nothing but that single, terrible fact.

I leaned close to Marco, so that only he could hear, and took his hand in mine. "Crayak is *not* going to have him."

Marco nodded. He squeezed my hand. "You got that right."

"Okay, it's unanimous," Rachel was saying.

"But not till I get a chance to pack some clothes, get some things, okay? In other words, you Drode piece of dog doo, not yet, okay? Not yet! Not yet!" she yelled.

But she was yelling it to a large creature that seemed to be made entirely of steel.

CHAPTER 6
Rachel

"Not yet!"

It was dark.

It was raining.

And there was a very large man, on a very large horse, wearing very steel armor right in front of me.

"Rrr-EEE-hhhuhhuhh! Rrr-EEE-hhhuhuhuhh!"

The horse reared up and pranced in surprise. Hooves as big as dinner plates flailed. I had appeared right in front of it. We both had. Cassie was beside me.

"Oh, man!" I said. "I knew he'd do this!"

I glanced around in the dark. I didn't see the others. No surprise. I barely saw the knight on his horse. A damp, sputtering campfire away through the trees cast just enough yellow light to outline the almost dainty metal boot in the ornate stirrup, the long steel shank of his thigh, the chain-mail glove that gripped the reins, the elbow joint, the helmet with a pointed visor decorated with elaborate filigree. The red-and-gold logo on his shield.

And, of course, the sword that hung at his side in a red scabbard.

"The Tin Man?" I said under my breath.

"Uh-uh. I don't think so, Toto," Cassie said.

My feet were sinking into mud. And it occurred to me that sitting on a horse in the pouring rain was probably not a good time. The red knight was very likely to be cranky.

The armored man got his horse under control. Barely.

Then, he drew his sword.

SCHWOOF!

Definitely cranky.

"*Sorcières!*" he roared, his loud voice muffled by the visor.

"What?" I asked.

"I don't know," Cassie said nervously. "I don't exactly speak French."

"French? He's speaking *French*?"

"Like I know?" Cassie said, a little shrilly. "I've only had half a year. I got a B minus on my last test."

The knight rattled off a string of French. And then he pointed his sword right at me.

I held up my hands, palms out. "Chill," I said. "No problem here. Just a couple of wet girls from the future out for a walk. Nice meeting you, we'll just be on our way. No-ay problem-ay."

"Where are the others?" Cassie wondered.

"*Anglaises?*" the knight shouted.

"Hey! I know that word. It means 'English,'" Cassie said, sounding pretty pleased with herself.

"*Anglaises! Espionnes!*"

"Spy!" Cassie translated, nodding her head like she was proud. "*Espionnes.* Espionage. Spies. English spies. That's what he said."

I swiped my hand back over my forehead to get some of the water out of my eyes. It didn't work. I looked at Cassie. "You know, Cassie, when he says 'English spies,' I don't think it's exactly a compliment."

"À moi! À moi!" the red knight yelled, still holding the sword toward me.

Suddenly there came the sounds of hooves pounding mud. I glanced back and saw a vague shape pelting toward us. I caught a glint of steel armor and green fabric. And now, from all around us, men were running, sloshing, pounding through the mud.

"This is looking bad," I said.

We were surrounded. We were getting more and more surrounded. And in the black night I saw fire-limned swords and axes and lances.

"I don't know where or when we are," Cassie said. "What are we supposed to do?"

"How about stay alive?"

"Morph? For all we know, one of these guys is Visser Four. We can't morph!"

"You have another idea?"

The new horseman arrived like thunder. He splashed up and reined in. The hooves of his horse threw up mud and clumps of soggy grass. And now there was a very long, very sharp spear leveled at us from behind.

"They see us morph, they'll kill us," Cassie whispered.

"It's dark," I said. "Besides, they'll figure we're something supernatural. Probably run away."

I had absolutely no confidence that I was right. But I wasn't going to stand there and be shish-kebabed without a fight.

The new knight, the one with faint traces of green on his mud-spattered, battered shield, took over questioning us. His visor was up, revealing a dark hole where we could have seen eyes and a mouth if it had been light enough.

The green knight rattled off a rapid-fire question. We shrugged. I don't know if he noticed that

I shrugged with somewhat larger shoulders. Or that my skin was turning leathery and gray.

"*Ce sont des sorcières anglaises*," the red guy explained.

"We're English," Cassie translated. "I'm thinking maybe 'witches.' English witches. Spying English witches."

"English?" the new knight demanded.

"Well . . . American actually," I said.

"Yes, we're *English*," Cassie jumped in, speaking pointedly to me. "Totally *English*, Rachel, because what would a couple of *Americans* be doing here in France in the *past*, right? Back when people still wore armor and stuff? I don't think so."

"Ah. Right. English," I agreed, though my voice was thickening as my tongue began to grow in my mouth, and my upper lip melded into my nose and began to grow.

"Rachel!" Cassie said. "You're not . . ."

But I was. And right then, the French guys noticed.

The green knight yelled something I don't think Cassie will ever be able to translate, and then he lowered his lance to horizontal, spurred his horse, and charged.

CHAPTER 7
Cassie

"Look out!"

Rachel tried to jerk aside, but she was growing fast and her legs didn't exactly match the rest of her. She was a tangled, horrific mess of mismatched body parts.

I leaped toward the spear.

Missed!

I fell into the mud at the horse's feet. It was huge, looming high over me, draped with embroidered fabric, its head encased in jointed steel armor.

Half by accident, half by instinct I kicked the horse's knobby left knee.

"Ahhh!" I thought I'd broken my foot!

The horse stumbled.

The spear's point missed Rachel by millimeters. The green knight plowed on, right over me! Hooves jackhammered the mud around me.

"Rachel!"

The horse's chest slammed Rachel hard. But Rachel was bigger, now. Not as big as the horse, but not small enough to be knocked over, either.

The green knight backed his horse off, cursing and yelling.

The red knight spurred his own mount. He raised his sword high over Rachel's lumpy head.

Sproot!

Sproot!

Two immensely long, curved white tusks exploded from Rachel's face.

The sword whizzed as it slashed in a downward arc.

CHUNKTH!

Sword blade hit tusk!

<Hah!> Rachel exulted. <Now let's see how bad you guys are! Maybe you want to teach me my place!>

I walked back, stumbled, fell on my butt in inches of mud, picked myself up and slunk back into darkness, away from the melee. Out of the firelight.

I was no use to Rachel. Not as a human girl.

I was already morphing to wolf as fast as I knew how.

Where was Jake? Where were the others? Why were Rachel and I left to deal with this alone?

Was Jake still alive?

<Come on, tough guys. What, are you scared?> Rachel raved.

The two knights were having a hard time trying to control their horses. The mud sucked at their hooves. The bizarre new smell of elephant sent their horse brains reeling.

The foot soldiers had stayed out of the fight so far, which was all that had saved Rachel. If they had charged, she'd have been hacked apart. But the knights hadn't given them a signal. And I guess the concept of initiative for average guys was still a few centuries in the future.

The fire blazed up suddenly.

Pounding hooves! A flash of steel, coming down hard!

<Aaaahhhh!> Rachel cried as a three-foot cut appeared in her shoulder.

The two knights spurred past Rachel and turned to come back at her. One with now-bloody sword raised. The other with lance lowered.

"Rrrachllllrrr!" I tried to scream a warning. But my mouth was pressing outward, filling with long teeth.

I was only half-morphed. No matter. There was no time!

I bounded forward and fell, facefirst, into the mud as my legs twisted and shrank.

I staggered up, but my arms were morphing to front legs. Fingers gone and replaced by pads.

Time wasted!

The knights charged.

Rachel bellowed.

The horses whinnied in fear but kept going.

The knights passed Rachel on either side.

It happened in an instant.

<Argghh!> Rachel cried in pain, even as she twisted and threw her trunk sideways.

I could see the spear protruding from her flank. There had to be two feet of sharp steel blade and wood shaft buried in Rachel's side.

I saw a horse, riderless, disappear in the darkness.

Then I saw the red knight. He was held high in the air, a thick, powerful trunk wrapped around him like a python. Chain-mail hands clawed futilely at the trunk. He screamed something to the men below him.

"Hreee-EEEEEEE-uh!" Rachel bellowed in elephant rage.

The green knight was wheeling back around. He pulled his sword from its scabbard.

About half the foot soldiers were running away gibbering and yelling. But the others were coming to the knight's aid, charging at Rachel.

I tried to stand up but suddenly I was staggered by a blow on the back of my neck. Wolf instinct rolled me over, almost as fast as a cat.

THUNK!

A spear impaled the ground beside me. I saw a wild look on the face of the foot soldier above me. He tried to yank the spear free.

Now, I was fully wolf. And the man realized he wasn't going to yank that spear out in time.

I bared my teeth and snarled.

He turned and ran, yelling something over his shoulder. I didn't know what, but I had a pretty good idea that it included the French word for 'werewolf.'

Rachel bellowed, "Hrrrr-EEEEE-yah!"

I was up. And now I had all the wolf's enhanced senses. I could smell the elephant. I could smell the horse. I could smell sweat and filth and moss and mud.

I could smell fear.

And in a flash of lightning I saw a scene from a medieval nightmare.

The remaining knight in wet, muddy armor, shield gone, astride a massive horse festooned in dirty green livery, was charging, sword held forward. Toward what he must have thought was a dragon.

And the dragon — the African bull elephant — was charging straight for him, tusks thrust out, trunk high in the air holding the squirming, helpless, screaming red knight.

It was no contest. Maybe with a lance the green knight might have had a chance. Not with a sword. And not against Rachel, who was going to slam his brother knight down on him with the force of a dropped safe.

I scrambled out of the mud and ran, full tilt at the knight. Padded feet flew!

A foot soldier loomed up before me, crossing himself frantically as he waved an ineffectual sword at me. I snarled. He fell to his knees.

I leaped, soared, landed lightly on the man's bowed head, kicked off again, and sailed through the air.

I hit the green knight.

He fell away. He hit the ground, shoulder first, then facedown in the mud. I landed on top of him. Many tons of gray flesh went plowing by, tree-trunk legs motoring easily across the mud.

The knight tried to get up. The mud held him captive.

<Stay down, you idiot!> I said in frustration. <You want to get stomped?>

I heard new footsteps running. And my wolf

senses detected a new smell. One that was definitely out of place in this era.

I was pretty sure it was salsa.

I looked up and saw Jake and Marco.

Jake. Still alive.

<Which one of you ate at Taco Bell today?>

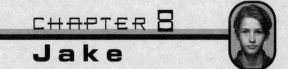

CHAPTER 8
Jake

It was not a good situation.

I was seriously annoyed.

One knight was stuck in the mud. A foot soldier was on his knees praying and quaking. The other knight was being held up by Rachel's trunk about six feet in the air.

<Oh. Hi, Jake. Hi, Marco,> Rachel said.

<Hi,> Cassie said.

<We were . . . uhhh . . . well . . .>

"So, there we were, suddenly appearing in the middle of a bunch of tents full of guys wearing armor," I said conversationally. "Naturally we figured we'd better lie low. Not attract attention. Not cause any trouble."

<Are you really mad?> Rachel asked.

I leaned over and grabbed the green knight's arm. Marco grabbed the other and we yanked hard, trying to get him up out of the mud while he cursed us in French.

"I figured I'd try the subtle approach," I said. "But, of course, that's just me. It hadn't occurred to me that what I should do is morph into elephant and STOMP PEOPLE INTO THE MUD!"

<You *are* mad.>

"Why would I be mad? Just because at the very moment I'm thinking 'Cool, we snuck past the guards,' I suddenly hear an ELEPHANT?!"

Marco laughed. "Half the guys back there in the tents are wetting themselves and babbling about dragons and devils."

<Hey, *they* started this,> Rachel said.

I sighed and rubbed my forehead. "Rachel?"

<Yes Jake.>

"Do you think you could put that guy down and demorph so we could get out of here without wiping out ten thousand future French people who might be descendants of these two guys?"

<You know, he stuck a *spear* in me,> she grumbled.

I helped the green knight get to his feet. "Sorry," I said. "How do you say 'sorry' in French?"

"Sorreeee?" Marco offered. "Ah em verreee sorreee."

"That's very helpful, Marco," I said.

Cassie had demorphed. Now Rachel put the red knight down gently and began to demorph as well. I saw the red knight heading toward a dropped sword.

"Hey! Uh-uh," I said. "No no no."

He stopped.

Just then Tobias swooped down through the trees. Another bird of prey was with him. Ax, in harrier morph.

<See, Ax? Told you it was Rachel. Any time you hear a bunch of screaming and see people running, you're going to find our girl Rachel somewhere close by.>

"Very funny," Rachel said. "*They* started it. Cassie: Tell them who started it!"

"Okay, look, we're all together. Let's get out of here before we draw the whole French army down on us," I said. "There must be a couple hundred guys back in that field up there."

<More than that,> Tobias said. <I don't see all that well at night but I saw more like thousands behind us. Campfires all over the place. And some more over in front of us.>

<Two armies?> Ax suggested.

"And us between them?" Marco said. "Great."

"Two armies? What war? What year?" Cassie asked.

I shrugged.

"The green guy there speaks English, I think," Rachel said.

I looked at the knight. Despite the armor he wasn't really much bigger than me. Standing in the mud without a weapon he wasn't too intimidating. "Excuse me, sir, can you tell me what year this is? And who's fighting this war?"

"I do not parlay avec *weetches*," the knight said in haughty, heavily accented English.

Marco stifled a giggle.

"I'm not the *weetch*." I pointed at Rachel. "Those two are the witches. I saved your life."

"Hey!" Cassie objected.

The knight thought it over for a moment. "It ees the year of our lord fourteen-fifteen. The forces of the Roi de France, hees highness royal Charles VI, under command du Constable de France and Princes of the blood royal, are here *unis pour* . . . to repel *l'envahisseur,* Roi Henri five of England, who has laid claim unjust to the throne of France."

"French and English? Whose side are we on?" Rachel asked.

"We're not on anyone's side," I said. "We're just here to make sure Visser Four doesn't mess with whatever is supposed to happen here."

"But we don't know what's supposed to happen here," Cassie pointed out.

<That's a definite problem,> Tobias said.

"Okay. First thing: We don't do anything till we find Visser Four. And when I say don't do *anything* that would include squeezing French knights with our trunks till they pop open like an overboiled hot dog."

"He has on armor! He barely felt it!" Rachel said hotly.

"Let's get airborne," I said. "What we're looking for is anyone who doesn't belong. Also we're looking for the Time Matrix. Ax?"

<Yes, my Prince.>

"What does a Time Matrix look like?"

<I do not know.>

"Better and better," Marco muttered darkly.

"Okay, just look for . . . just look. And remember one thing: We are just as likely to mess up the future as Visser Four is. So be careful. Cover this whole area. If we're some kind of quantum echo or whatever then Visser Four must be nearby. Anyone spots him, we'll need to move fast and hard."

I looked around at all my friends. I tried to make eye contact with each as I repeated. "Fast and hard. You understand? This guy has the most dangerous weapon ever created. We can't let him get away. His personal history ends here."

CHAPTER 9
Marco

The sun was barely up. Gray dawn.

We flew. We looked at stuff. We demorphed. We remorphed. We flew some more. The sun was coming up and we still had not seen anyone who we thought was Visser Four.

However, I'd seen some really cool armor. Mostly on the French side. The English guys looked pretty raggedy. And about half of them seemed to have serious digestive problems. Every five minutes you'd see one of the English soldiers run off into the bushes and . . . well, let me put it this way: What they did you don't really want to see, especially with high-power osprey eyes.

I was over the English camp for about the twentieth time. The head guys, including this guy I thought might be the king, were attending an old-fashioned mass. You know, in Latin.

Their *third* mass. Which made me wonder if they had any hope of winning. I mean, one church service, maybe. But three? That's not a sign of confidence. That's more like "I'll be there any minute now, Lord, so have Saint Peter make up my bed."

The guys themselves, knights, soldiers, archers, and so on, were a nasty-looking bunch of humans. No one looked like they'd washed their clothes any time this century. Faces were dirty. Teeth were rotted — and I mean yellow-and-black, gnarled-looking rotted. They were pompous, swaggering knights and whatever, who had literally four and a half teeth in their whole head.

And speaking of heads, here's a clue: You didn't want to have really good eyesight and see these guys' hair. We're not just talking fleas. We're talking lice. And not one or two. Every head was like a Manhattan of lice. A Hong Kong of fleas. There were crawling little bugs packed onto some of these guys like fans at a Phish concert.

And skin? Scabs, rashes, bumps, boils, warts, things you thought might be beetles stuck on their faces but that were actually moles.

It was pockmarked city. Virtually every face looked like someone had fired a shotgun at it. Deep holes you could almost stick a finger into.

Smallpox, of course.

It was not an attractive crowd. English or French, it didn't matter, except that the French had more horses and cooler armor.

Ax wheeled through the sky, twenty feet above me, closer to the French lines.

<I do not mean to insult your ancestors, Marco, but if the Yeerks had arrived in this era they would have left to find some other species to infest. These humans have all the parasites they could possibly support.>

<Oh yeah? What were Andalites like three, four hundred years ago?>

<We were relatively backward technologically,> Ax sniffed, <but we had managed to discover cleaning agents. These humans are universally filthy.>

<They are . . . Hey! That's it! Jake! Rachel! Everyone! These guys are all dirty and lice-ridden and pockmarked!>

<It took you three hours to notice that?> Rachel demanded. <You're a genius, Marco.>

<Well, duh, Rachel, guess who *wouldn't* be all skanky?>

<Visser Four! Of course!> Cassie said. <He has a twentieth-century body! Twenty-first century. He won't have smallpox or lice or bad teeth!>

<That's it,> Jake agreed. <Look for someone clean! That'll be our boy.>

The sun was rising above the horizon now. The mass was breaking up. It didn't look like they'd have another. I guess three were enough.

The guy I thought was probably the English king was hanging out with some of his boys, all laughing very loudly the way people do when they're scared peeless but want to look cool.

I took a look at him. No, he did not have a twenty-first-century body. He was about as skanky as anyone. I checked out his boys, a bunch of burly-looking troublemakers. I guess they were his main knights, but if it hadn't been for the chain mail and the swords you'd have figured them for a bunch of Mafia hit men.

They weren't all buff like some Schwarzenegger action hero. Most were beefy, even fat. I doubted any of these guys had ever even heard the word *salad.* But they weren't fat fat, they were like, "Ah-hah! Your blade merely penetrated my belly fat and one kidney! A flesh wound! Have at you, sir!"

These boys were trouble.

And now the king was talking to his troops. He jumped up on a fallen tree and started bellowing and waving his arms like a politician or a football coach.

I couldn't hear everything he said, but the basic idea was, "Men, we're outnumbered, but we're here for a good reason, which is that I want to be king of France, so let's go kick some French butt and we'll all be mighty pleased with ourselves on the off-chance that we actually survive."

Basically the same kind of heroic nonsense we Animorphs tell ourselves before we go into battle.

Then, quite suddenly, I saw him.

Not a knight. One of the archers. He was carrying a bow and a quiver full of arrows. His clothes were the same uniform as the other archers: a sleeveless leather jacket decorated with steel studs over a chain-mail shirt; and pants that looked like they'd been sewed together by seamstresses with only three fingers and a ballpoint pen for a needle. He was with a bunch of archers moving toward the French lines.

<Got him!> I alerted the others. <Over there at the tree line. He's an English archer.>

<On our way,> Jake said. <Stay cool. We need the right moment.>

<I think this battle is getting ready to start. If you want to buy some popcorn and Raisinets better hurry.>

The English were definitely moving. The French, who had to outnumber them four-to-one, waited very calmly. In fact a lot of them were off riding around, talking to each other, drinking, scarfing snacks, making out with women, and gambling.

Between the two forces, a narrow, muddy field hemmed in by trees on both sides.

<The English are gonna get stomped,> Rachel said. I could see her bald eagle wheeling down toward me, turning wide circles.

<Maybe not,> Jake said thoughtfully. <The field is so narrow. The French can't get all their guys into the action.>

<Want to lay some money down?> Rachel asked.

<This is probably not why we're here,> Cassie pointed out. <Probably the idea was not to place bets.>

<Why are we here? That is the question,> Ax said. <What is the significance of this particular historical event? How would a change at this point in the time-space continuum cause the changes we observed?>

<I don't know,> Jake admitted.

<Neither does Visser Four, most likely,> Cassie said. <All he knows about humans came from the mind of his host body.>

<Swell,> I said. <It's the blind leading the blind down history's . . .>

I stopped talking because I saw something no bird ever, ever wants to see. Ever.

I saw about two thousand guys notch their arrows, draw their bowstrings back to their ears, and suddenly elevate straight up.

Straight up at me.

CHAPTER 10

Marco

I was staring down at about two thousand arrow tips, and two thousand guys squinting up at me along the arrow shaft.

<Uh-oh.>

Flit! Flit! Flit! FlitFlitFlitFlitFlitFlit!

The air was filled with arrows. It was like some weird backward hail. It was a wall of arrows!

Flit!

<Aaaahhhh!>

An arrow passed clear through my wing. I banked hard.

Flit!

<They're shooting at me!> I yelled. There was a sharp pain in my wing, and blood streaked my

feathers. The wing was weaker, but I could still fly.

<Get outta there!> Rachel yelled.

<Gee, do you think?!> I said frantically.

I beat wing but now it was like every idiot on the ground was trying to murder me. Already, they were reloading. But I was hauling. Hauling not exactly in a straight line because one wing was dragging, but I was moving. I headed more or less along the front of the English lines, trying to stay in no-man's-land. One thing I knew for sure: I didn't want to try and cross directly above the English troops.

Unfortunately, that was a bad insight. The archers were on both ends of the line, in the woods! I was heading straight for another couple of thousand archers!

Ahhh! I tried to turn. I tried to haul. I would have run on air if necessary.

Arrows snapped into place, up came the bows, and . . .

FlitFlitFlitFlitFlitFlit!

Clean miss! I was out of the way, and now I could watch where the arrows were heading. Down they came.

The arrows arched toward a column of Frenchmen on horses. Maybe three hundred guys, many loaded up in fabulous armor. Some in less-than-fabulous armor. But all yelling from behind their visors, all with long lances leveled.

The French cavalry went straight for the archers. The archers were behind a lame wall of spikes angled out toward the horses. Unfortunately for the English, their spikes wouldn't stay up in the mud.

But the spikes weren't the important issue. The important issue was the arrows.

FlitFlitFlitFlitFlitFlit!

Thousands of arrows, all shooting up, all arching, all seeming to hang in the air. Thousands of these arrows just sort of waiting, poised at the top of their arc. A fly could not have gotten through that wall of arrows.

Down and down to stick in French arms and necks and shoulders and heads and thighs and faces, and all of a sudden what was happening below me was not a joke anymore.

FlitFlitFlitFlitFlitFlit!

Arrows flew again, tracking the approaching column of rowdy, disorganized cavalry.

The main knights seemed almost invulnerable at first with all their armor. Even their horses were armored along the back of their necks and over their heads. But the arrows were so thick that they found their way into the narrow slits in knights' visors.

Men were dropping. Horses were dropping.

If I'd stayed one second longer, avoiding the arrows would have been like avoiding raindrops in a thunderstorm.

If I had stayed a second longer I wouldn't just have been shot. I'd have been a pincushion.

Now the screaming started. Guys with arrows sticking through their necks, into their stomachs, out of their sides, all fell and crawled and stood up and fell again. And it wasn't just the men. Horses were screaming, too. And that's not a sound I'll ever forget.

The cavalry fell back. They didn't look good. They plowed right into their own lines, practically riding down their own people.

The English kept coming. Looking a little more sure of themselves, too. Like maybe *two* masses would have been enough.

I tried to find Visser Four again. I looked for that weirdly clean face, the weirdly white teeth. And that saved my life. Because I saw now that the archers were forward, half in the woods, and they had shifted their aim.

Suddenly, the arrow barrage had changed direction.

<Aaahhh!> I yelled, spilled air, and plunged like a rock. I saw the English archers release their strings.

I saw arrows fly!

Right. At. ME!

FlitFlitFlitFlitFlitFlitFlit!

Hundreds of arrows arched toward me as I dove toward the ground. Hundreds of arrows, some so close I felt the breeze from them, blew above me.

I raked, opening my wings to catch air. But now my injured wing failed. It collapsed, seemed to break in half, and down I went at impossible speed.

Flump!

I hit mud, beak first. I maintained consciousness for about a half second. Passed out. Woke up to hear Jake yelling, <Marco! Marco! Get up!>

CHAPTER 11
Rachel

Down went Marco.

I saw him stick, literally *stick*, in the mud. I was high above and to the right, off the main field. I was in bald eagle morph — the only one of us nearly big enough to drag an osprey up out of the mud.

I dove.

<Rachel! No!> Jake yelled.

<I can get him!> I had Marco in plain view. A crumpled little wad of dirty gray-and-white feathers in the middle of what was, by the standards of 1415, probably the most dangerous piece of real estate on Earth.

I fell like a stone. No, like a missile, because

I was under control, directed, aimed with a dozen tiny movements of tail and wingtip.

<Break off!> Jake yelled. <The arrows! The arrows!>

FlitFlitFlitFlitFlitFlit!

The arrows!

I opened my wings wide, spread my tail feathers, pulled my talons up, and did an impersonation of Wile E. Coyote trying to stop in midair after he's just run off a cliff.

It didn't work much better than it does for Wile E.

The arrow barrage flew. Two or three missed me by millimeters, but most were well below me.

As soon as the arrows were by, I folded my wings, making the smallest possible target, and dropped again toward Marco.

<Marco! Wake up!> Jake yelled.

I swept down, barely avoiding hitting the mud myself, and dug my talons into Marco's back.

<Hey! Ow!>

<Complain later, we are outta here!>

Only we weren't outta there. I flapped with all my strength and managed to drag Marco about three feet through the mud. But there was no way we were getting airborne.

FlitFlitFlitFlitFlitFlit!

The arrows flew again, this time far overhead. And then I heard a bloodcurdling sound. The roar of battle lust from hundreds of throats. Or maybe not so much battle lust as sheer terror.

I shot a look to my left. The English were suddenly running. Right at us. To the right: the French, running, galloping, and also doing some screaming.

We were about to be stomped by several thousand really unattractive shoes.

<What do we do?> I asked Marco.

<How do I know? I thought you were rescuing me!>

<Demorph?>

<And tell them what? We're neutral?>

The first wave of English troops was ten seconds away, still yelling, brandishing spears and swords, their boots making sucking noises in the mud. The French maybe twelve seconds away.

Then, suddenly, from the woods near at hand, a horse burst at a run, heading straight for us.

I knew that horse.

At least, I hoped I did.

<Cassie? Tell me that's you!>

<Get ready!> Cassie said.

<To do what? Birds don't ride bareback!> Marco yelled.

The English from the left. The French to the right. Arrows still filling the air above us. And a single horse kicking up dirt clouds and splashing through mud puddles as it came.

<Too slow!> Marco said tersely. <And she doesn't exactly have hands. How does she pick us up?>

<Oh, man,> I said, bracing for the attack.

In a flash, the English soldiers were all around us, yelling about Harry and England and just generally yelling. Thick, felt-shod, rag-wrapped feet stomped all around us.

Then, hooves.

Feet! Hooves! Someone tripped, facedown, landed beside Marco and me. At least I thought he'd tripped. Till I saw the short arrow sticking out of his chest.

It was the green knight. He lay on his shield and tried to breathe. I stared at him, unable to look away. Unable to stop myself from thinking that at least he wouldn't live to tell the story of the witch who became an elephant.

<Grab my legs!> Cassie cried.

<What?>

<Grab my legs!>

Brown horse legs were tall in a forest of shorter limbs. I sank talons deep into bone and skin. It had to hurt. But Cassie didn't complain. Marco did the same, and then we were off. Two big mud-encrusted birds of prey latched on to a horse's front legs as the horse tried to shove through a melee.

And the melee had just gotten radically worse.

Cassie, and we, were shoved by the force of the packed bodies around us, toward the French.

Now, battle was joined. There was no way out. I dug my talons deep. A horse might survive this hell of yelling, slashing, screaming, shoving, grunting, stabbing madness, but a bird is a fragile animal.

<Arrgghh!> I heard Cassie cry. I assumed it was the pain of my and Marco's talons.

But it was much more likely that the pain came from the spear that had been shoved deep, deep into her haunch.

Cassie stumbled. She fell, facedown. I disengaged just in time to avoid being crushed.

Then a foot came down on me. I heard the tiny bones in my back and wings snap.

It hit me then: I was going to die. Not Jake, me. Mine was the life Crayak would take in payment.

I was going to die almost 600 years before I was even born.

CHAPTER 12

Ax

<Cassie!> Prince Jake cried.

<They're down!> Tobias shouted. <I'm going in!>

<No!> Prince Jake ordered. <We don't need another body down there!>

The two groups of humans rushed together and began to attempt to murder each other by the use of edged pieces of steel in various shapes and forms.

Some of the humans rode atop horses. Some appeared to be wearing artificial skin made of thin sheets of metal.

It is one of the rare examples of artificial skin that makes any logical sense.

But I did not have time to ponder the question of armor. Cassie, Rachel, and Marco were wounded and very possibly dead.

Flying high above the battle, I caught only occasional glimpses of them. A struggling horse, lying on its side. Two birds. All ignored by the murderous humans around them.

At the same time, I was attempting to keep track of the movements of Visser Four. He had fired many arrows from the bow that was almost as long as his own body was tall. He had fired more slowly and with less skill than the other archers, but no one had seemed to notice.

And now, he was moving. Many of the English archers on both wings of the battle had laid down their bows and were drawing swords and daggers. Now I saw the disadvantage of the steel artificial skin: The archers, dressed only in cloth, and carrying light weapons, were able to move more nimbly through the mud. They were able to jump in and stab several of the armored knights through their visors.

But Visser Four was not a part of this slaughter. He had backed away from the battle into the trees. And now he appeared to be climbing a tall tree.

<Prince Jake!> I cried. <Visser Four is in a tree. I believe he is preparing to use his bow.>

<Forget Visser Four!> Tobias said hotly. <Rachel's down there! Rachel! Morph!>

<She would have to demorph first,> I said. <As a human she would surely be killed.>

<Shut up!> Tobias cried in anguish. <This can't happen! Ellimist! Crayak! Get us out of here! *Get us out of here!!*>

I was disturbed by the possibility that my friends would be killed. But there was nothing to be done for them. And our mission was to stop Visser Four.

I peered closely at his face. It was a normal human face. Perhaps with a bit more facial fat. He appeared to be of adult age, though young for that category. My estimate would be that he was twenty-five years old.

<Polar bears!> Tobias pleaded. <We morph to polar bears and rip into that mess down there! We can't just do nothing.>

<Cassie's down there, too,> Jake snapped. <And my best friend.>

<We have to do something!>

<Like what? Kill a bunch of innocent guys who should have lived? Those aren't Controllers down there. Those are human beings!>

I tried to stay focused on Visser Four. As I swept in a slow circle above the field of battle, I trained my osprey eyes on his blue human eyes.

They searched the crowd. Then, found what they sought. I tried to extrapolate, to follow the direction of his gaze. It was an inaccurate game at best. But I believed I saw what he was watching.

In the middle of the English lines was a warrior wearing a dented gold ring atop his helmet. Many men in armor were close to him. There were several bright flags near him.

<The human with the gold circle on his head,> I asked. <Is he important?>

<Gold circle?> Prince Jake asked in a frazzled, distracted voice. <You mean a crown?>

<Possibly. It is gold and formed into what may be an abstract floral design.>

<That's the king! The English king!>

<He will be shot with an arrow very soon,> I said. <Visser Four is drawing his bow and I believe he is aiming it at this king.>

<Get him!> Prince Jake yelled.

<I am too far away,> I said. <Only Tobias . . .>

CHAPTER 13
Tobias

<Rachel!> I yelled.

<Tobias! That guy's getting ready to shoot!> Jake said. <I can see him.>

<Tobias, I cannot get there in time,> Ax said with infuriating calm.

Both of them alike! All Jake or Ax cared about was the stupid mission. I could see Rachel and Marco, half-crushed by Cassie's horse body.

No! Wait! Not crushed. They were shielding themselves beneath her. They'd be crushed, yes, but maybe not killed. If I could get to the woods, morph to polar bear, come back, break through . . .

Insane! Jake was right. How many terrified soldiers on both sides would I have to kill? And how long would I last?

<Tobias!> Ax said. <It is now or possibly never!>

I looked down. I could see Visser Four through a break in the trees. I saw him from above. He was drawing his bow. Ready to . . .

Flit!

Too late! The arrow flew. Straight toward King Henry.

Straight into the back of a young French soldier who fell like someone had cut his legs off.

A miss!

Of course! Visser Four was no expert archer. And it was a tough target. The king's face was uncovered. That had to be the target. A professional archer could have done it from this range, but not a novice.

Still . . .

Visser Four drew his bow again. He aimed very carefully. And now the king was surging toward the very place where Rachel and the others lay.

Visser Four might not hit Henry. He might miss and hit Cassie or Marco or Rachel.

"Tseeeeeer!"

I spilled air from my wings, folded them back, twisted my tail to aim, and flew straight down.

Down like a rock.

I saw Visser Four's fingers begin to relax.

I saw the fingers release.

The arrow flew!

I opened my talons and twisted sideways to bring both talons into line.

Flit!

Fwapp!

Talon hit arrow. Right talon hit but didn't grip.

I blew straight down, my momentum carrying the arrow with it, canceling some of its speed. Left talon squeezed!

I felt the shaft slide through my grip. Thunk! My talons closed around the feathered ailerons.

It all took a tenth of a second. Then, I was carrying the arrow.

<Go, Tobias!> Jake cried.

I turned and saw Visser Four. He was staring at me with a mix of amazement and disbelief. And then, slowly, slowly on his face dawned recognition.

I could literally see his lips form the word.

The word *Andalite*!

<Not exactly,> I thought, <but you've got the basic idea. Jake? I think he's made us.>

<What?>

<Visser Four. I think it's occurred to him that normal hawks don't go around snatching arrows out of midair. And now, I'm going after Rachel and the others. Visser Four is your problem now.>

CHAPTER 14
Cassie

I was in agony. I was lying on my side, with Marco and Rachel half-hidden beneath me. The spear had penetrated deep into my side and all I could do was to try and remember my horse anatomy.

What had the spear hit? Not my heart, or I'd be dead already. My stomach? Intestines? Liver? Who could tell. But I knew that I was weakening. And I knew that if I demorphed, I'd leave Marco and Rachel exposed and helpless.

Not to mention the high likelihood that a superstitious fifteenth-century soldier would almost certainly kill the weird, twisting abomination I would seem to be in mid-morph.

We had to get away! But how?

The battle raged around us. The noise was horrific to my horse ears. Steel clanging against steel. The clank-clank-clank as crossbows were wound tight. Hooves and feet pounding in the mud, and landing, all too often, on bodies.

Men grunted with the effort of swinging their heavy swords and maces and axes. Men cried out or moaned as they were hurt. They staggered and fell, from wounds or from sheer exhaustion.

And all of this was all around me. On top of me!

This, I would later learn, was the battle of Agincourt. One of the great battles of history. Glorious. That's what people called it: glorious. Shakespeare wrote a play about it.

But I'm here to tell you there was nothing glorious going on. It was as glorious as murder.

<We have to get out of here,> Rachel said.

<How?> Marco demanded. <We move, we die!>

<Cassie's bleeding,> Rachel said. <She's bleeding all over me.>

<Cassie, can you stand?> It was Jake's voice. Coming from far overhead.

<I think so. Maybe. I don't know.> This wasn't my body. I didn't know for sure what it could do. I didn't know how badly it was injured.

<Well, get ready. The cavalry's coming,> he said. Then he added. <We hope.>

I tried to stand. My legs worked. But I was

weak. I couldn't roll enough to get up. Not without crushing Rachel and Marco.

<What are you guys doing?> Marco asked Jake.

<Well, this is the age of superstition, right? Witches and goblins and devils and all?>

<Yeah,> Rachel said.

<We're giving 'em a devil,> Jake said.

<A devil? What do you mean, a devil?>

Then, above all the clashing, yelling, horrific sounds of battle, I heard a new note. Screams of sheer terror. Screams like you'd hear from someone trapped in a nightmare.

Feet stampeded.

The king himself stood over me, recognizable for the dented golden crown on his head. He was staring off to the right. Gaping, mouth open, battle temporarily forgotten.

The knight he'd been fighting sagged to his knees and began crossing himself and praying. Battle lines fell back. The king thought about it for a few seconds and decided he didn't want to go one-on-one with what was coming, either.

And the devil — or what must surely have looked like a devil to these men of the fifteenth century — rode onto the field atop a magnificent warhorse.

<Am I seeing a Hork-Bajir riding a horse?> Marco asked.

The Hork-Bajir — Tobias, actually — came

charging straight toward us. Brave warriors, warriors who'd gone face-to-face in this battle, life for life, suddenly bolted. The forest of legs around me parted.

Rachel and Marco crawled out from beneath me. I rolled onto my side and struggled to my feet, woozy, weak, half dead, but not so dead I couldn't run a few hundred yards.

<Come on!> Tobias yelled, turned his horse, and led the way back off the field.

The horse said, <Hey! Watch the blades, Tobias!>

Marco and Rachel grabbed my torn and bleeding legs, and we made off across the horrible field. Over the bodies of dead and wounded, knights and peasants.

<Visser Four?> Rachel asked.

<Ax is keeping him busy,> Jake said. <But we have to hurry. Or he'll get away from us.>

CHAPTER 15
Ax

Visser Four ran. But he was merely a human-Controller. So there was very little chance of him outrunning me. I was still in harrier morph. I swooped through the trees as he ran.

Rising above the forest I could see the edge of a small village in the trees ahead. If Visser Four made it to the village it would be harder for me to stop him. There would be innocent humans about.

But as a harrier I could do very little to stop him.

Decision: Stay with the Visser and be helpless, or stop, demorph, and be able to attack?

The village, a collection of primitive human

dwellings with roofs apparently made of grass, was very close.

First: Keep him from the village.

I flapped my wings harder and easily caught up with the running, panting, frightened Yeerk. I turned in midair and plunged toward him, talons down and forward.

He looked up. Dodged to the side. Not fast enough. I felt my left talon catch the side of his head.

"Aaaahhh!" he cried.

I swept past and turned to come back after him.

"Andalite filth!" he screamed. Genuinely screamed. Pure, unfiltered hatred blazing in his blue human eyes.

He hesitated. I came for him. He broke and ran. But now there were other humans surging around us. A column of men on horses was blundering through the woods seemingly heading around toward the rear of the English lines.

But there were other humans, too. They were running from the battle. Running toward the village.

I could not demorph in plain view. The Yeerk must have known this. Now he stopped and put an arrow into the simple bow he used.

He drew the arrow back and let it fly. My harrier eyes were able to see that it was poorly aimed. It blew past and I did not even need to adjust my flight.

He ran again, and I followed. Suddenly we emerged from the edge of the wood. There was an open space between the forest and the village. There appeared to be some sort of crop planted there. Villagers were calmly harvesting, going about their busy work as though nothing was happening.

Possibly they were concerned that the battle or fugitives from it might trample the crop.

These humans barely looked up from their work as soldiers, archers, and knights on horses went running past.

Certainly they did not notice Visser Four. Or me.

I swept up to Visser Four and raked his head again, laying the scalp open. He grabbed at me, but missed.

"I'll kill you!" he raged.

<Surrender now, we have you surrounded,> I bluffed. But a Yeerk does not rise to Visser rank by being a complete fool. He laughed at my silly threat.

This was a pointless battle, I knew. In this morph I could injure him but not stop him. If I stopped to morph I could well lose him.

There were two large structures in the village. One seemed to me to be essentially military. A fort of some sort. The other had a large main building with a tall tower at one end.

It was into this building that Visser Four ran. Through a tall door.

The door had been open. He slammed it behind him. I flared my wings and pulled up, inches from smashing into the heavy-timbered door.

<Prince Jake!> I called in frustration. <Tobias! Marco! Rachel! Cassie! Anyone who can hear me, please answer.>

But there was no answer. We were far from the battlefield now. I was on my own.

How to enter the large structure? How to . . .

And then, in a flash, I knew why Visser Four had returned here.

<The Time Matrix!> He'd hidden the Time Matrix in this structure! I had minutes, maybe not even that.

I landed on the stairs leading to the front door. I began to demorph. My Andalite stalk eyes began to writhe up and out of my feathered head. My fleshless bird legs grew meat and muscle and true bone. I rose, growing taller by the second. But all too slowly!

Hands! I needed hands!

Tiny, limp protrusions began to grow from my chest. My forelegs. But my wings remained wings. No fingers appeared.

<Prince Jake!> I yelled again.

Visser Four was going to escape.

<Prince Jake! Rachel! Cassie!>

Now, at last, fingers! But too weak, too delicate and unformed to turn the heavy iron handle on the door.

"Aiiiieeee!" someone screamed.

A human. Perhaps upset at the sight of an Andalite struggling to emerge from . . .

"*Tuez-le! Tuez-le!*" a new voice screamed.

"*Tuez-le!*" Now it was a chorus. I twisted one stalk eye, only now beginning to work.

There were half a dozen humans. Some were soldiers. Others not. The ones who were soldiers brandished swords. The others held huge forks made of sharpened wood.

I was quite sure they were not welcoming me to their town.

<Prince Jake!> I cried. I lurched on half-formed legs to reach the door. My weak fingers closed on the handle.

The angry villagers attacked.

CHAPTER 16
Tobias

<Prince Jake!>

Jake was already running. We'd both heard a faint cry from Ax. This one was louder, clearer. We must be running in the right direction.

<Cassie! Rachel! Marco! Get clear, then demorph, get wings and follow!> Jake said. <Come on, Tobias, we're the cavalry again.>

I leaned down over Jake's flying mane, which allowed room for my spiked tail. The horse morph was huge. He'd acquired one of the chargers of a dead French knight. It easily carried my Hork-Bajir weight. Probably not much different from a man in full armor.

We raced through the trees. Behind us, the battle resumed. I guess in 1415 having the devil show up was a fairly normal occurrence. Nothing to stop a battle over. Not for long, anyway.

We burst suddenly into the open. Ahead of us, a village. Peasants scattered as we plowed along the dirt street, knocking wheelbarrows over, sending unwary pedestrians sprawling.

It wasn't much of a village, I guess. A kind of not-impressive fort and a church. The church was on a square. The square was full of runaway soldiers, the wounded, the scared, and a bunch of regular villagers.

All were converging on the church steps. Half a dozen had hold of an animal that might have been a blue deer with a scorpion tail, but for the fact that it was half-covered in gray feathers.

<Ax?> Jake asked.

<Yep,> I said.

<We're going in!>

Jake redoubled his speed and went plowing straight into the crowd. I rode till he was stopped by the compacted bodies around us, then I stood up on his back and leaped.

Hork-Bajir are naturally arboreal. Meaning they live a lot of their lives in the trees. So they can jump pretty well.

I jumped. I sailed over the heads of outraged villagers and slammed into a wooden door so thick and sturdy it might as well have been a tree.

WHAM!

I landed on Ax.

<Ahhh!> he yelled.

<Sorry!>

<Visser Four is inside!> Ax said, sticking to business despite the fact that the nearest villager was trying to stick him with a wooden pitchfork.

I clambered away from Ax and snatched the pitchfork out of the guy's hands. If they didn't already believe I was a devil, they sure did now.

<Come on!> I yelled. I grabbed the door handle, twisted it easily, and shoved back on the door. Ax and I together spilled inside. I slammed the door shut behind us, snatched up a four-by-four and popped it into the iron slots, barring the door.

We were in a church. I was a seven-foot-tall creature with horns and a spiked tail holding a pitchfork. And I was in a church.

I looked at the altar. I looked at the terrified priest who was shaking so badly he couldn't cross himself.

<Sorry,> I said to the priest. <It's not what it looks like. Sorry,> I added, looking at the altar. <Boy, is this the wrong morph in the wrong place.>

Ax was fully Andalite now. Which didn't help our appearance one bit.

<Visser Four!> Ax said. <I don't see him.>

<Me neither.>

<The Time Matrix! He has almost certainly hidden it here. If he reaches it, he will escape.>

Then . . .

BONNNNNNG!

A distant ringing.

<The bell tower!> Jake cried from outside. <He's in the bell tower.>

I shot a look around. Stairs. There had to be . . . <Over there!>

We ran. Ran for the stairs and bounded up them two, three at a time.

The stairs twisted in a tight circle. My big Hork-Bajir feet were twenty sizes too big. I slipped and skinned my knees on sharp stone. Ax leaped over me and raced ahead.

Above us, a wooden platform blocked our way. There was a trapdoor.

FWAPP!

Ax's tail snapped and cut a slice out of the trapdoor. I shoved up beside him.

<Allow me,> I said.

I drew back my Hork-Bajir fist and rammed it straight upward. The trapdoor slammed back on its hinges.

I pushed myself up and through. Not possible for Ax.

And there, before me, was the deadliest thing ever created.

It was a shimmering, featureless globe. Almost as tall as I was. And Visser Four had his hands pressed against it, a look of concentration on his face.

He smiled at me.

"So. The Andalites pursue me still," he sneered. "I was careless. I did not expect to be pursued. But I'll be careful now. Yes. And you know what? It's better this way. I have the power now! I have the POWER!"

I lunged.

The globe shimmered. Visser Four grinned.

My blades flashed.

On emptiness.

CHAPTER 17
Jake

"Where'd that dang horse come from?"

"Don't reckon I know, Tom."

"It's *Sergeant*, you clodhopper. How many times I got to tell you that? He must belong to one of the officers. He's a beauty, he is."

The horse was me.

I'd been standing outside the church as Ax and Tobias raced to catch Visser Four. Obviously they'd failed because I was no longer outside the church.

Now I was standing in the middle of a press of men, all shuffling more or less forward.

Forward was toward the muddy bank of a river.

It was dark. Night. Cold.

The horse morph had been bred for northern

European winters so it wasn't suffering too much. That didn't change the fact that it was cold.

The sky was dark. The kind of dark you don't see in a world filled with street lamps and porch lights.

Clouds hid the moon and stars. So dark that I could barely see the two or three guys closest to me. I saw the river only because the bank was outlined in white: Ice floes were crunching into the shore.

I heard the sound of wood on wood. A hollow, random sound. Boats bobbing together in the river current.

The ground had probably been snow-covered. But now it was mud churned by hundreds, possibly thousands of feet.

One thing was sure, at least: This was no longer France. The men around me spoke English. The accent was strange, kind of as if you had a bunch of country folks trying to speak with an English accent.

"Don't much favor the look of them trees over yonder," a man said. "Whole troop of Hessians could be back up in there."

"If they's Hessians I guess the general would know," another man answered. "'Sides, some of our boys is already acrost."

Hessians. The word meant something to me. Something.

What?

I'd heard it before, I was sure of that. Maybe the guys around me were English or maybe American, but either way I'd never heard of any war with Hessia. Hessland. Whatever.

Where were the others?

<Marco? Cassie? Anyone?> I called out in cautious thought-speak.

"Someone get this here horse out of the way!"

A hand searched in the dark for my bridle. I didn't have one. I backed away, knocking a man down.

I turned and shouldered my way through the men. Whoever had been trying to grab me must have lost interest.

<Rachel! Tobias! Anyone hear me?>

No answer. Maybe they weren't near enough. Maybe they hadn't been dragged through time, yet.

Maybe they were no longer alive.

Where was I?

There was a murmur of anticipation from the men around me. "General's comin'. Guess we'll be getting along, now."

"They say as we're late and the Hessians be waiting for us. They's a whole army of 'em in Trenton. I know. My sister's husband is from Trenton. Says them Hessians is right tigers in a fight."

"What do you know about any tiger, Elias, you ain't never seen a tiger, have you?"

"Shut your cakeholes, you lot," an authoritative voice snapped.

I stopped moving. Couldn't go any further for the men pressing in all around me, making a lane for the general.

He walked by quickly with half a dozen well-dressed men trailing him.

I never would have recognized him. Not from any of the paintings I'd seen. Certainly not from his face as it appears on the one-dollar bill. But the men were whispering his name.

"Washington."

He was a big guy. He wore a long buff-colored coat over tight white pants that stopped below the knee. His hair was white. *Of course,* I thought, *that's a wig.* Rich people or important people all wore wigs in those days. These days.

George Washington. Father of the country.

"You know who that is?" Marco asked.

He'd sidled up beside me, out of nowhere.

<Jeez, Marco. How long have you been here?>

"Got here about five minutes ago, dude. Heard you calling. Couldn't answer, though. I'd already demorphed."

I turned my big horse head to aim one eye at him. <Where'd you get the clothes?>

"Not exactly clothes," Marco muttered. "A blanket with a hole for the head. The boots are cool, though."

<Where did you find boots?>

He shrugged. "You think it'd change the course of history much if George Washington was to lose his extra pair of boots?"

<You stole George Washington's shoes?>

"Hey, it's freezing, all right? Not all of us happen to be horses at the moment."

I heard someone make a not-too-subtle remark about lunatics joining the ranks.

<Marco, stop talking to me. People are noticing. They think you're nuts.>

Marco fell silent. And then, <Jake? Cassie?>

<Rachel? Is that you?>

<Yeah. I'm in owl morph flying above an army down by some river with some boats. Guys are carrying old-fashioned rifles.>

<I know. Marco and I are down here in the middle of it. I'm the horse. Marco's the one wearing Washington's boots.>

<No way. *George* Washington?>

"Jake, tell her 'No, *Guido* Washington.'"

<Marco would like me to pass along a sarcastic remark,> I said.

<Wow. Washington. Is this the Delaware? Is he crossing the Delaware?>

<I guess so. I mean, I've heard Washington

crossed the Delaware, but I don't know what it means.>

<This river is the Delaware. The Delaware River,> Rachel said. <I mean, come on, even I know that!>

<Why is he crossing the Delaware?>

"To get to the other side and see the chicken," Marco whispered.

<Is it just us?> Rachel asked. <I just got here like three minutes ago. I demorphed and morphed, and now I don't see Cassie or Ax or Tobias anywhere.>

"Oh good, it's starting to rain," Marco complained.

<Rachel? Don't waste time looking for the others, look for Visser Four.>

<Gotcha.>

From down by the water came raised voices. Someone not exactly yelling, but definitely mad. A low-key laugh seemed to travel through the army.

"General's giving 'em hell."

"What for?"

"What for? Are you simple? We're late, that's what for. We'm supposed to be acrost and march over to Trenton afore first light."

Trenton. Hessians. Washington crossing the Delaware.

<Visser Four is after Washington,> I said.

"Yep," Marco agreed.

<We have to get out of here. I have to demorph. Rachel? Find Washington. He must be the target. Stay on him. Whatever you do: Protect George Washington.>

"There's three words you never thought you'd say," Marco said with a low laugh.

CHAPTER 18

Rachel

Protect George Washington.

Right. No problem. I was an owl.

The army was loading into the boats. Not enough boats, from the look of it. They must have already pulled across the river once; there was a group of a couple hundred over there.

What had started out as rain had quickly become sleet. The weather was miserable. And it was clear that the men on the ground thought so, too.

Many of them wore little more than rags. Rags were wrapped around their feet. They weren't quite as skanky as the French and English at Agincourt but they were close. If they had fewer fleas and lice it probably had to do with the fact that it was too cold for fleas to breed.

I drifted above them, my wings coating up with sleet every time I stopped flapping them for too long.

I kept Washington in sight. He had to be Visser Four's target, just as King Henry had been. It made sense. Visser Four's plan was to remove influential people from history. It was the obvious thing to do: no Washington, maybe no United States. Maybe the Revolution fails and everything changes.

But why King Henry and Agincourt? What would have happened if Visser Four had managed to kill Henry?

<Doesn't matter,> I muttered. Some English king was one thing. This was the Father of our Country. The first president of the United States. No one was going to take him down.

But we *could* use more help, I realized. Marco and Jake were trapped down in the mass of men. Jake was still in horse morph, although I saw Marco leading him away toward the woods, presumably to demorph.

That was still just three of us. Where were . . .

<Yah!> I yelped in surprise. It was sheer accident that I happened to be looking when Cassie popped into existence about fifty yards down the riverbank, just beyond range of the colonial soldiers. She was human. She must have been left in 1415 long enough to demorph.

<Cassie! I see you. I'm in owl morph. Here's the deal: Washington is crossing the Delaware, and yes, I mean *the* Washington.>

I saw her look up. Night is meaningless to an owl. Even this night.

I saw her mouth form the words "George Washington?"

She couldn't see me, of course. <Yeah. George, National Daddy, that's me-on-the-dollar-bill-with-a-city-and-a-state-named-after-me Washington,> I said. <Jake figures Visser Four is going to try and smoke him. They're getting ready to load him up, I think. George, I mean. Yes, he's heading for a boat.>

Cassie made a sinuous motion with her hands. A swimming motion.

<Dolphin? Yeah. Good idea.> Cassie in the river, yeah, that would help, maybe. But Visser Four could be beneath any of the hundreds of hats I saw below me. All he needed was a musket and a clear shot. He could already be taking aim . . .

Jake and Marco reemerged from the trees. Both human. And somehow Jake now had a blanket over his head and some rags wrapped around his feet.

I didn't know how that had happened. But I guess if Marco could find a way to rip off Big George's extra boots . . .

Still they had to be cold as they plowed through the crowd of men, rushing to reach a boat.

<Jake? Rachel? Is anyone else here, or am I the only one watching George Freaking Washington climbing into a boat?>

Tobias!

<You recognized him?> I demanded.

<Of course I recognized him,> Tobias said. <That's The Man! Are you kidding?>

<Is Ax with you?>

<Yeah, the both of us popped up just now. We're across the river. I'm still in Hork-Bajir morph. Think maybe I'd better demorph. What's the deal?>

<Jake and Marco human, getting into a boat. Cassie, mid-morph a dolphin, about to get into the water. Me, I'm flying around enjoying the delightful weather.>

<There are armed men over on this side,> Ax interjected.

<I don't see 'em,> Tobias said. <Hork-Bajir eyes, man.>

<Those are good guys,> I said. <Guys have been going across for a while now. I don't think they have enough boats.>

<Ah,> Ax said. <They seem to be very alert.>

<I guess they would be. They're on their way to go kick butt in Trenton.>

<Ah,> Ax said again. <But . . . > He hesitated, as if something was bothering him.

<It's okay, Ax, it's a good thing they have guys over there already,> I said, reassuring him. <Nothing to worry about.>

CHAPTER 19
Marco

We got into a boat. Turned out not to be all that hard. No one was all that anxious to climb on board for the trip across an icy, raging river in the middle of a sleet storm.

Can't imagine why.

"Ah, yes," I muttered to Jake, "the Love Boat takes a detour to hell."

"My feet are freezing," he answered, eyeballing my feet. My warm, dry feet. "Too bad the Big Guy didn't have a third pair of boots."

"They wouldn't fit you," I said. "Not your size."

"Uh-huh."

There's a very famous painting of Washington crossing the Delaware. It shows George standing up in the middle of this boat like one of the lifeboats from *Titanic* and looking all determined and Father-of-the-country-ish.

Two things wrong with that.

One, the boats were low-sided, flat-bottomed, rocking, spinning, swamped, water-up-to-your-ankles pieces of junk. Not that you could even feel your ankles. Unless you had boots on.

There were too many wet, mad, depressed, shivering, scared men and boys packed into too few boats in the middle of a hurricane of sleet on a river that was a rush-hour expressway of gigantic chunks of ice.

Sleet was piling up on my head. There was sleet on my shoulders. Sleet in my eyes, sleet freezing into a crust of ice on my knees, sleet on my bare fingers, fingers numb, numb till they would barely move and you had to think about unbending them.

On top of all this, the guys were not thinking so much about how they were on a mission to create a great democratic nation. They were mostly concerned with the fact that the sleet was getting down the barrels of their guns, and into the flintlocks, and how wet gunpowder might as well be Bisquick.

That was the first thing wrong with that painting.

The second thing was if George had been a

big enough idiot to want to stand up in the middle of all this, his men would have figured he was a lunatic and turned around and learned to enjoy crumpets.

If you worked at it, you could not create a more miserable little boat trip. Guys rowing like mad. Using poles to keep the icebergs from turning us into a bunch of badly dressed Leonardo DiCaprios.

"That's the guy," Jake said. He was looking toward the boat that rode the current a dozen or so feet away to our right. Or starboard, I guess.

Washington's boat.

I thought at first he meant he'd spotted Visser Four. But he was looking at Big George.

You know, it's dumb, I guess. I'm not some big "wave the flag" guy, you know? But that man over there, huddling down in his coat while the ice crusted his hat, that was George Washington.

It was hard to digest.

I twisted my head, dislodging some of the slush.

"Like Tobias said: The *Man*," Jake said. "No him, no us maybe."

"Yeah. And Visser Four could be in his boat right now."

Jake nodded. "Rachel's on it."

"Hey, we're almost there. Gee, I hate to see this pleasure cruise come to —"

Ka-PopPopPopPopPopPop!

A horizontal line of flame erupted, blinding in the darkness. Twenty, thirty, who knew how many ancient muskets, all firing at once, a disciplined volley.

I couldn't see the damage done. But I heard the cries.

"Turn back!" someone screamed.

A second volley!

Ka-PopPopPopPopPopPop!

Again, exploding powder drew that awful horizontal line.

"We're betrayed!"

"Turn back!"

"No! Forward!"

Our boat began to turn, but lost its way and simply wallowed as men lurched back and forth in panic.

On the far shore, no longer so far, the ancient flintlock muskets opened fire again. Fingers squeezed on triggers. The hammer, with its chip of flint, slammed down against steel.

The spark ignited the powder in the flashpan. It made a small coughing sound.

Then the main powder charge ignited.

Pop!

A ball of lead the size of a marble flew.

But not one, single gun. A mass of guns. All firing at once.

Fifty, sixty, a hundred explosions!

A hundred balls, flying, singing through the air.

Thunk!

The man sitting in front of me fell back. His head dropped on my lap.

"Aaahhh!" I yelled.

Thunk!

An oar was blown in half.

Thunk!

A hole appeared in Jake's forehead.

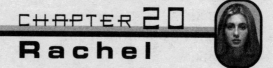

CHAPTER 20
Rachel

<Nooooo!>

Jake fell straight back without a twitch or a movement. Simply collapsed. A puppet whose strings had been cut.

Marco lunged across the boat to grab him.

I saw the hole. It was centered in Jake's forehead.

The back of his head was gone. There was no possible question. He was dead.

In a flash, I understood.

It wasn't the advance elements of the colonial army that Ax had seen on the far shore. It was the Hessians, moving in to ambush.

Visser Four had enlisted allies in this assassination.

Another huge crash as the Hessians fired another volley.

More men died. Half the men in Jake and Marco's boat were dead or injured. I could see the Hessians. Neat, orderly rows of green-coated soldiers.

Hessians. German mercenaries working for, fighting for the British. This was not even their war.

Men were trying to turn Marco and Jake's boat. Trying to head it back, away from the guns.

A volley. And now, deeper, booming explosions, as a cannon added its voice.

BOOOM!

A boat blew apart.

It was slaughter.

Another boat capsized, spilling men into the water.

Boats slammed into each other.

The dead bodies went over the side to slip beneath the black water.

Men were trying to shove Jake over. Lightening the boat. Marco fought them, but they knocked him back.

<Cassie!> I cried.

<What?> She was alarmed, she'd heard the guns. But she didn't know.

<Cassie . . . Jake . . . his body! You have to get it. You can't let it . . . >

<Oh, my God!> she wailed.

I saw her surface. She was downstream. She fought her way back up. She would find Jake. She would. But there would be so many bodies for her to look through.

I saw him go under, sinking. An ice floe glided over him.

I saw Marco. Yelling. Crying.

Saw Washington's arm get hit by a bullet.

I didn't see Visser Four. But I knew he was there. This wasn't the way it had happened. Washington's men had surprised the Hessians. The battle had been won by the Americans.

Someone had warned the Hessians. Someone had told them where to wait.

My head was swirling. All so impossible. Jake. Impossible!

<Save Washington!> I said.

<What do we do?> Tobias asked.

Do? I didn't know! <Attack!> I blurted. <The Hessians! Attack them!>

<Rachel,> Ax said, <these Hessian humans are only doing what —>

But my doubt was gone. Attack. Yes.

<They killed Jake,> I snapped. <And they're trying to get Washington. They could kill Marco. They die! Do you hear me, Andalite? They killed your prince. *Do your duty.*>

CHAPTER 21
Ax

Tobias was in his own hawk body. I was in my own Andalite form. Cassie was in the water. Rachel in the air. Marco was in a boat, under fire. And Jake, my prince, was dead.

Only I was in a position to attack the firing troops. Only I could avenge Jake's killing.

I ran through the woods over muddy ground, slick from falling ice. The trees were dark. Thorns and brambles ripped at me.

Crayak had taken his payment. But that did not mean the dying would end.

Was Rachel right? Should I attack these humans?

My form alone would breed panic among them. But they were professional soldiers. Some would break and run. Others would not. I could use my tail to knock some unconscious.

But they would rally. Their officers would direct fire at me. Unless I could remove their officers quickly enough . . .

I would have to kill. Kill men who should have lived. Not only take lives, but wreak havoc throughout human history.

But wasn't that already happening?

This battle should never have taken place. Men were dying who should have lived.

What should I do?

Ka-PopPopPopPopPopPop!

Another volley. The left of the Hessian line was only seconds away.

Marco might have died in that last volley. Or, if he lived still, he might die in the next.

I raced for the nearest soldier. He didn't see me. I whipped my tail forward.

FWAPP!

The flat of my blade hit the side of the soldier's head. The soldier fell.

FWAPP!

Another dropped, unconscious.

A third turned, saw me, froze, unable to pull the trigger of his primitive firearm. I knocked the gun from his hand.

But now an officer was yelling, and more soldiers were turning, turning toward me, leveling their guns, fingers on triggers . . .

I ran. Pushed off with my hind legs.

Ka-POP!

I leaped.

I sailed over the heads of the Hessians as their explosive fire ripped the air below me. I landed hard, tripped, staggered, caught myself and veered toward the officer.

He drew his sword. He was brave. But no human is fast enough to evade an Andalite tail. His sword would not stop me. My blade would remove his head from his shoulders.

No choice. The killing had to stop. Marco . . . the human called Washington . . . no choice. My stalk eyes looked down the dark, wet slope toward the river. Most of the Hessians were still firing. Men in the boats were screaming.

I drew back my tail.

FWAPP!

CHAPTER 22
Cassie

Bodies sank.

Bodies floated.

Bodies rushed by, caught up in the current. Staring eyes goggled, dead.

Blood. Everywhere.

<Jake!> I cried his name. Maybe, somehow. Somehow he could hear. Somehow Marco was wrong.

I surfaced to suck in air, surfaced to escape the horror below the boats. But the surface was worse still.

Bullets, fired in horrifying volleys, continued to chip boats and bones. Men cried out. Men fell into the water.

It was slaughter. I couldn't see Marco. Or Washington. Were they alive?

<Jake!>

I echolocated, firing clicks that bounced off hulls and ice floes and arms and legs.

<Jake!>

I bumped into a body. It turned.

<Oh, my God. Oh, my God, Jake. Jake! Jake!>

I got beneath him and started to push his body along toward the riverbank.

<Come on, Jake, come on with me. I'll get you out of here. Oh, God! Oh, God!>

Bullets ripped through the water. I swam on, oblivious, through the freezing water. I could sense the riverbank before me. Just a few feet away. Just . . .

Gone!

Jake's weight was no longer on my back. The riverbank was gone. Boats . . . gone.

Sunlight shone down through the water. It was daylight!

<Jake! Jake!>

I echolocated. No, there was no body, nothing but a school of fish.

No! Time jump!

I surfaced.

The sun was out from behind clouds. A gentle breeze blew. And, moving on that breeze, sailing ships. Dozens! Maybe more.

They filled my horizon in every direction, towering, tall, three-masted wooden ships, with vast white sails billowing, flags flying.

Jake was not here. Not *now*.

I felt sick. Jake. Dead. But not here, and not now.

Visser Four had escaped again. And we, like a tail on a kite, had followed, helpless.

<Jake!> I cried.

No. He wouldn't answer. He would never answer again.

And now, another battle was preparing. Another place where Visser Four could twist human history. Maybe the human race deserved it.

My mind was nothing but pain now. Nothing but guilt.

Marco and I were going to save him from Crayak. We were going to keep him alive. But in a flash, in a battle that should never have happened, in a war I hadn't even paid attention to in school, he'd died.

I couldn't feel this pain. Couldn't. It was a hole inside me. It was a twisting knife.

But beneath my own wailing, lost human mind, was another. The dolphin . . . yes, the dolphin knew only that the sea was full of fish, and that was good.

CHAPTER 23
Tobias

Flying after Ax, heart hammering, wings whipping up and back, up and back. Racing, zooming wildly, recklessly through tree branches I could barely see. My mind gone, gone at the realization that it had happened.

Jake. It couldn't be. It didn't fit in my brain. It was impossible!

I spotted Ax. He was ripping into a row of Hessians. Down went one. Another.

He leaped! Straight over them, landed, and headed for the officer.

He was going to kill the man. Rachel had told him to.

No, it was wrong! This Hessian officer wasn't

responsible. Crayak. That's who had killed Jake. That's who'd set up this hopeless fool's errand.

<Get us out of here!> I yelled. <Crayak, Ellimist, whoever, get us out of here! We quit!>

No answer.

Ax headed for the Hessian officer. The man had a sword in his hand. I could yell to Ax to stop.

I could . . .

<Aaahhhh!>

A wall of white rushed toward me, billowing, huge, filling the sky!

I banked hard.

No, it didn't fill the whole sky. I could see sky. It took a few seconds for me to understand.

A sail!

A large, square sail, and below it, another. Above it another as well. The wind blew them toward me. They killed the breeze for me, blocking it. I had to flap hard to stay ahead.

I banked away, outside the path of the sail and caught the breeze.

Time jump. Visser Four had moved again. He'd done the damage he could do.

Below me was the tapered oval of a wooden ship. Three masts, each taller than a tall tree. Ropes, some of them as thick as someone's leg, stretched everywhere, from mast to mast, from mast to deck.

Men in uniforms with gold braid and boots

stood over other men in off-white dungarees, bare chests, and bare feet.

I looked around. There were ships in all directions, seemingly forming two rough lines. Two lines stretched across miles of calm seas. The two lines were moving with unhurried, stately grace to an intersection.

Every ship bristled with cannon.

<Marco? Rachel? Ax? Cassie?>

No answer. They could be miles and years away. I saw a lone dolphin keeping pace with the big ship below me.

<Is that anyone? Marco? Is that you? Cassie?>

I was talking to a dolphin. I was alone.

I circled down to the ship. I kept pace with it, me and a bunch of seagulls.

The ship was very ornate. The stern was slightly bowed, with gilt-edged windows opening on a room with a table. I flapped to move closer in. I approached till I could see most, if not all of the cabin.

Then, with a few quick flaps I was inside, suddenly in still air. I landed on a table covered with charts and maps and papers. My talons tore fragile paper.

There was a quill pen. An inkwell. Leather-bound books. In English. I could read the words on the chart. And I could make sense of the map showing the position of the ship.

We were in the Atlantic Ocean. Close to Spain. There was a point of land. It was labeled Trafalgar.

I dropped down beneath the table and began to morph. If I was going to find Visser Four I needed to be able to move around the ship.

And I was going to find Visser Four. Crayak might be the great evil, but it was this one Yeerk who had killed Jake.

And I was going to find him and see how well he could swim.

CHAPTER 24
Marco

Ax was beside me. Andalite, but right there beside me.

It was gloomy where we were. Maybe night, maybe not. There were murky candles somewhere, out of direct sight.

We were in a world of wood. A low wooden ceiling made up of planks hung on humongous, elephant-leg timbers. There was a wooden floor beneath my bare feet, a grate, actually. Ax's hooves kept slipping through the holes.

The floor was tilted, moving slightly from semi-level to definitely not level.

Around us, forming a sort of wall, enclosing an oval space, were ropes, piled high, almost to the ceiling. Ropes as thick as Mark McGwire's biceps.

<Where are we?> Ax wondered.

"A boat. Ship of some kind," I said. "Down below. Morph to human, man."

<Perhaps not just yet,> Ax said. <We appear to be trapped. Enclosed behind this barrier of rope.>

He was right. We were trapped.

I tried to push at a coil of rope. My fingers were trembling.

"Sorry," I said.

<Sorry for what?>

I leaned against the wall of rope and threw up.

Jake had slipped right under the water. Right under. They'd shoved him over the side and I couldn't stop them.

A hole in his head. Like someone had put it there with a drill.

I'd told Cassie we could protect him. I'd agreed: Crayak wouldn't have him. But it had happened so fast. One minute, nothing. The next minute, death everywhere. No arguing, no heroic actions, no nothing. It had taken a millisecond.

And now . . . what could I do for him now? Nothing. No one could help him. His parents . . . he would never come home. What could I tell them? What could anyone tell them? I climbed up on the rope and peered out through the narrow gap. I saw two men, both with backs to us. They were wearing rough dungarees that looked like they'd been made out of canvas. Stiffer than new jeans. One was an Asian guy. The other white.

The darker man was carrying a small barrel. The white man walked up behind him, produced a sort of short wooden club, and slammed it down hard on the other man's head.

He clubbed the Asian man again as he fell.

My mouth opened to yell. But Ax's Andalite hand was over my face.

<It's *him*,> Ax said. He had managed to get his stalk eyes high enough to see.

The white guy — Visser Four — hefted the barrel and carried it out of our sight.

"We have to get out of here!" I hissed, pulling Ax's hand away. "Morph to something small enough to —"

FWAPP!

TWANG!

Ax whipped his tail, again, again, again, and each time another loop of the rope cable parted.

<This is quicker. I am very tired of being too late,> Ax said.

"Got that right, man."

Visser Four was no longer in sight. Ax began to morph to human.

"Catch up when you can," I said. I took off in

the direction Visser Four had gone. A hallway going left and right. A stairway going down. Which way?

I looked down. A partial footprint, outlined in red.

Blood. From the man Visser Four had clubbed. I followed the trail down, down to a deck still darker and gloomier. And smellier.

I saw him quite suddenly. He was hunched over, waddling, carrying something heavy, low to the ground.

The barrel. Something was pouring out of it. It looked like liquid. No. A dark powder.

Gunpowder!

The Controller was laying a gunpowder trail so he could ignite the trail, run, and blow up the barrel.

He wasn't ready, yet. Neither was I.

I began to morph. It was a morph I'd done many times before. So I was used to the way my face turned rubbery. The way coarse black hair sprouted from every inch of my body except my face. The way my shoulders and neck swelled to ludicrous proportions. The way muscle layered onto muscle.

I'd been a gorilla before. But this was different. I savored every powerful muscle and sinew and steel-beam bone. I was going to enjoy using them.

<Hey,> I said.

The Controller who'd been Visser Four spun around.

I swung a fist the size of a football.

BOOOM!

The deck jumped!

Something shockingly powerful had hit the ship. My blow missed. Visser Four bolted.

<Not this time!> I yelled and went after him.

I didn't know where I was, or when I was, or who was driving the ship. So I didn't know who was going to see a gorilla racing around, and I didn't care.

Visser Four had made a fatal mistake. This was a ship. There were only two ways off it: Swim, or use the Time Matrix.

He could lead me to the Time Matrix, or he could die trying to outrun me.

CHAPTER 25
Rachel

"Lieutenant, sir!"

"Silence! Stand by your guns, men!"

"But, sir: Look!"

The thing the lieutenant was being invited to look at was me.

I was human, wearing an outfit that was definitely not appropriate, and standing on the open upper deck of a very large sailing ship. I had simply appeared. One minute I'd been in the woods behind the Hessians, having demorphed, getting ready to morph to grizzly. Then . . .

The lieutenant was a relatively young man, maybe twenty-five. Beside him was another person in uniform, probably no more than thirteen years old.

On either side of us were knots of tense men standing around huge, old-fashioned cannons. The cannons were aimed in the direction of another ship moving closer and closer.

The lieutenant, the kid, and the twenty or so men closest to me all gaped.

"B'Gad! It's a girl!" the lieutenant exploded.

"A stowaway!" a man with a scar said.

"She'll catch her death in that rig."

The kid whipped the hat off his head and performed a bow. "Shall I escort the young woman below?" he chirped hopefully.

"No, mister, you shall not. You will present my compliments to the captain and the admiral and inform them that we have a stowaway aboard."

"A rare beauty of a stowaway," the young guy said, leering and blushing.

He ran off, looking back over his shoulder as he stumbled his way to the raised platform farther back. A deck of some sort.

"All right, men, you've all seen a female before this. The Frenchman is over there! Stand by your guns. Steady, men, wait for the order."

The men went back to their guns, but with frequent looks over their shoulders. I ignored them. I was looking for a face with fewer missing teeth and no scars. I was looking for —

"FIRE!"

BOOOOM!

A huge explosion. The sound alone could have killed a person with a weak heart.

It was as if every cannon on Earth had fired at once.

The cannons leaped back on their clumsy wooden carriages, and snapped hard against thick ropes that held them in place. Smoke billowed up all along the side of the ship. I don't know how many cannon had fired but it was a lot. Thirty, forty, fifty, I don't know, but the concussion felt like a punch in the head. The noise left me half deaf, ears ringing.

Seconds later . . .

BOOOOM!

This time the smoke was from the French.

The railing not two feet from me blew apart. Huge splinters flew. A man was down, screaming.

The gun crews were already at work, swabbing, drawing the guns back with brute force, carrying round, steel cannonballs forward, manhandling them into the barrels of the cannon.

I barely noticed the man who shot up through a hatchway behind me. But I definitely noticed the gorilla who was after him.

"Marco!"

Visser Four ran. Marco followed.

I didn't hesitate. I raced after them both.

There were shouts of dismay and amazement from crewmen. Roared orders from officers. A red-coated soldier, a marine I guess, tried to cut Marco off. Marco pushed him aside with enough force to send him sprawling.

But two more red-coated marines and a sailor lunged and grabbed Marco, slowing him down. Visser Four bolted toward an open door. Then he stopped. Very suddenly.

A flurry of russet feathers, a flash of talons. Visser Four staggered back, clutching his face.

BOOOOM!

The cannon fired again.

BOOOOM!

The French answered.

A cannonball passed so close by my face that I felt the breeze. More men were down. Pandemonium! A gorilla, a hawk, a girl in a leotard, all racing, chasing a man with too-clear skin and too-white teeth while blue-coated officers bellowed, red in the face with rage, and scarlet-coated marines and dungareed sailors formed a freak-show chase scene.

Visser Four jumped and grabbed a handful of rigging. He was strong and agile. His stolen human body had belonged to a young unsuccessful actor. He swung himself up a sort of complex rope ladder.

It was a smart move. Tobias couldn't get at

him without risking being caught in the maze of ropes. And as strong as Marco was, gorillas are not fast tree-climbers.

<You're dead!> Marco raged, shaking off a pair of marines.

Visser Four glanced down then kept climbing.

Now the cannon were no longer firing in regular volleys. French and British alike were firing as fast as they could. It was a mad race of death. Which crew, British or French, could pull a ton of cannon back fastest? Who could swab the red-hot barrel, who could ram in the canvas bag of powder, the wadding, the cannonball, wrestle the cannon back up snug against the port, and aim it, all while being fired on by cannon and muskets?

Not my problem. Not my war. My war was with Visser Four.

I started to morph. Not grizzly. Not elephant. Marco had chosen the wrong weapon. This wasn't a job for brute force.

Rough brown fur began to grow from me. I didn't wait for the morph to be completed; I moved.

"Come back here, you!" someone yelled.

I was running. Bare feet on tilting wood that had been sprinkled with sand to sop up the blood.

BOOM! BOOM! BOOM!

Cannon fired. Sweating crews worked feverishly. Smoke choked my throat and stung my eyes. The ships were now within a few feet of each other. It was simple violence, hammer blows, hammering, hammering, hammering, as timbers shattered and cannon were blown off their mounts, and sails and masts and rigging fell, and men were torn apart.

The wind tore a rip in the curtain of smoke. Tobias! I saw him clearly, flapping hard to get out from under a large falling spar.

Crowded onto platforms high on the masts, marines fired feverishly down on the French. Visser Four swung up and around them, unnoticed.

I grabbed a rope. The sailors were incredibly agile, racing up and down the masts and ropes to shift the sails, to replace ropes that had been shot away. Visser Four himself wasn't bad.

But now I was a chimpanzee. The human hasn't been born who can touch a chimpanzee in a tree.

Ka-Pop! Ka-Pop! Ka-Pop! Muskets fired.

I swung up into the rigging and shot straight up at a speed and with an ease that made even the most graceful sailor look like a lumbering ox.

Up and up, hand and foot, hand and foot, effortless. Visser Four was above me, heading higher. Then, he looked down and saw me.

I enjoyed the fear in his blue eyes. I loved the fear in his eyes.

<That's right: You are all mine.>

Sudden silence. The cannon had stopped firing.

CRUUUUUNCCCHHH!

The two ships crumpled into each other. Grappling hooks flew, snagging ropes and spars and railings. The two ships were lashed together. British sailors began to pour over the side, rushing with wild cries onto the French ship.

BOOM!

The French had swiveled some small cannon to face the onrushing Englishmen. Half a dozen men fell like they were bowling pins.

And worse, from my point of view, the French had a couple of small brass cannon mounted on swivels on one of the mid-mast platforms. They were firing into the rigging.

Ping!

The rope I was holding parted. I fell! My left hand reached out and snagged another rope. Effortless. This was my world. This was my environment!

Visser Four was as high up as he could go, the junction of the highest spar crossed the mast. He was clutching the mast.

<Now where do you go, Yeerk?> I asked him.

"Get away!" he cried in a shrill voice.

<I don't think so,> I said. <Your personal history ends right here, right now.>

"No! Let me live and . . . and . . . the Time Matrix! You know you want it!"

<Where is it?>

"You'll never find it without me!" he said.

I laughed. <It's a ship. It's only so big. I'll find it.>

"You can't kill me, Andalite," he begged.

<Oh, but I can,> I said. <You killed someone I love.>

I shot up the mast, hand over hand. Three seconds and I would —

Falling!

I was falling, straight down, faceup so I could see half a chimpanzee still clinging to the mast.

Falling, spinning now, the realization slow in seeping into my dying brain: I'd been blown in half.

Darkening eyes saw Visser Four crowing, laughing and —

CHAPTER 26

Tobias

The chimpanzee fell to the deck. A hundred-foot drop.

The cannonball had separated head and left shoulder and arm from the rest of the body.

<Rachel! Demorph! Demorph!>

No answer. I knew. I knew. There would never be an answer.

Visser Four slid down the mast, grabbed a rope connecting to the foremast, and slid, screaming at the pain from the rope burn.

<NOOO!> I cried again.

<Tobias!> Marco yelled from down below. <He's heading for the Time Matrix! He'll get away!>

<She's dead!> I cried.

Ka-BLAM!

<What? Who's dead? Cassie?!>

<Rachel,> I cried. <Didn't you see? Rachel!>

<Oh, God, oh, God!> Marco wailed. <It's not just Jake! We're all going to die!>

<Cassie! Ax! Where are you?> I yelled. I dove to intersect Visser Four.

He had reached the foremast. Marco was pushing through anyone who got in his way, trying to cut him off.

I dove, weaving through ropes, around masts and spars and men. Visser Four grabbed a vertical rope and slid. I could see the blood trail he left on the rope.

His feet hit the deck.

I flared my tail and swept my talons forward and ripped his right ear.

"Aaahhh!"

I caught a head wind and came back around in a tight turn. He stepped off the edge of an open hatch and dropped to the deck below. He stood up and ran. I dove after him, down into darkness.

Now I was at a disadvantage. It was cramped, with low ceilings and wounded men being carried below.

I flew hard and wild, but I couldn't gain on the ever-receding figure. <Marco! I need help! He's heading forward!>

I turned a tight corner. Wham! Into a wall. I hit the deck, stunned but not unconscious. Left, right! Gone!

<I lost him!>

<I see him!> Ax yelled.

<Ax! Where have you been?>

<I had morphed to human and was injured. I am demorphed now, and following the Controller.>

I got airborne with great difficulty. No head wind, no tailwind, no lift, and a ceiling crowding down above me. It wasn't a place for a bird.

I flapped and landed, flapped and landed. Then down, down a stairway, left and . . .

An Andalite blew by. I followed him.

We erupted into a small room. A barrel of what could only be gunpowder was lying against one curved wall. The hull. A trail of gunpowder led from the barrel through a small door.

Ax and I raced for that door. And there, inside, stood a shimmering, six-foot globe.

And Visser Four. He was holding a flintlock pistol. Cocked. But not aimed at us. It was aimed at the gunpowder trail.

He grinned a grin made grisly by the fact that it seemed to continue in a red slash that went up to his ear.

"Nice try, Andalites."

He fired. The powder burned.

The Time Matrix disappeared. Visser Four was gone.

The powder trail burned and spit and crackled as it went around the corner.

I looked at Ax. He turned a stalk eye on me and said a word he must have picked up from humans.

<Get that barrel!> I yelled.

<What?>

<It's a bomb, Ax-man. The powder trail leads to a barrel of gunpowder. If it reaches it, BOOM!>

Ax hesitated only a second. Then he ran. I fluttered after him. Marco plowed into the room.

Ax swung his tail. FWAPP!

The blade cut the powder trail just an inch from the barrel. Unfortunately, Ax's tail blade struck a spark. The remnant of the powder trail blazed anew.

<Oh —> Marco began to say.

CHAPTER 27

Tobias

Quiet. That's what I noticed first. It was so quiet. No cannon. No muskets. No screams.

I opened my eyes.

I was at the base of a tree. It was fall. The tree was red and gold. Magnificent.

I staggered up onto my talons. I'd been time-yanked. I'd made it! The others?

I looked around. No battle. No armies. I saw big buildings. Old-fashioned, stone buildings. My first thought was that it was a college campus.

No one else. No Marco. No Ax. No Cassie.

No Rachel or Jake.

Was I the only one left alive?

Then I saw guys walking by, all wearing sports coats, all carrying books.

I looked beyond them, using my hawk eyes to see through windows, into the classrooms. Had to be a college. The kids were too old to be in high school. Although they looked strange: short hair, crew cuts, even. And something else: They were almost all men.

The professors were exclusively male. Here and there was a girl student. But not many. And then I noticed something else that took even longer to register: Everyone was white. *Everyone.*

It wouldn't be easy spotting Visser Four here. His host body was white. And about as clean-cut as these people.

I called out in thought-speak. <Ja —> No. Not Jake. And not Rachel, either, unless there'd been some kind of miracle.

<Marco. Ax. Cassie.>

Was that all of us? Four left alive? And maybe not that. Maybe fewer. Maybe just me.

I felt sick. Rachel had not survived. She'd been dead before she hit the deck. Ax and Marco had been a split second from being blown up. And Cassie? I'd not seen or heard her at all.

<Ax! Marco! Cassie!>

We were getting ever more spread out across time and space. The resonance, this weird trailing of the Time Matrix was scattering us. Like an echo that grew ever more faint.

I landed in a tree and began to morph. I

needed to be human to . . . But no. I'd stand out way too obviously here wearing stupid morphing clothes.

First, I needed to be able to pass. If this was a college there'd have to be a dorm nearby. Where there was a dorm there was clothing.

Hawk eyes made the search easy. I found a dorm, and a window open to the fall chill. Ten minutes later I emerged human wearing a pair of baggy slacks and a white shirt and a V-necked sweater.

I couldn't do anything about my shaggy hair. Everyone would just have to deal with it.

I walked downstairs from the dorm, carrying some student's books. I could only hope no one would recognize my clothes as belonging to someone else. But with everyone looking like Stepford Students and wearing the same thing, how would they tell?

I opened one of the books. It was stamped: Princeton University. The publishing date of the book was 1932. That didn't mean this was 1932, but it did mean it wasn't any earlier than 1932.

It was a history book.

I whipped it open and scanned the contents. Revolutionary War. Revolutionary War.

No listing. But there was a listing under "Rebellion, Colonial."

I flipped to the pages. I found what I was looking for.

"The rebellion collapsed following the disastrous attempt by rebel leader George Washington to attack British-allied Hessian troops. Rebel troops attempting to cross the Delaware River were ambushed by Hessian allies who had been alerted by a local resident. The result was a massacre. Washington was mortally wounded, dying three days later while in British custody."

"*Local resident.*" Visser Four.

I sucked in air. I'd been there. How long ago? A hundred and fifty or so years ago? Or just an hour ago?

They didn't mention the death of an unknown rebel. A boy with a bullet in his brain.

I scanned the contents page again. Another word jumped out at me. "Trafalgar."

No mention of Rachel. No mention of gorillas or hawks or a chimpanzee. The entry simply explained that the British Navy had been defeated by a fleet made up of French and Spanish ships. Admiral Lord Nelson was killed when his ship, *Victory*, was sunk by an explosion below the waterline.

I shook my head. I didn't know how it was *supposed* to turn out. I'd never even heard of Trafalgar. Didn't even know what war it was.

I closed the book. I raised my eyes and saw the flag flying from a tall pole. It was pale blue, with a small British Union Jack filling one corner.

Princeton University was not flying the American flag. No one was flying the flag of the United States. There was no United States. What there was in its place, I didn't know.

But the United States of America had died on a sleet-stormy night on the Delaware River.

Suddenly, down a wide alleyway between tall buildings, a dolphin appeared.

CHAPTER 28
Cassie

The battle had raged around me, above me, up on the surface. I didn't care.

I was a dolphin. I was happy being a dolphin. I could reach down into the dolphin's natural reservoir of childish glee, its sense of adventure, its basic contentment, and escape the awful pain.

Jake was gone. I couldn't think about that. Couldn't accept it. It was a burning hot coal that I couldn't touch.

Around me the cannon boomed. Stupid. All of it, so stupid. From the cosmic battles between Crayak and the Ellimist all the way down to this battle, this stupid, stupid waste of life.

I headed away from it. Just away. Away from the pain and the stupidity of it all.

Escape, Cassie. Run away.

No.

I couldn't. I'd tried that once. Tried to run away from war. It hadn't worked.

I argued with myself, plowing through the water, trying to find a way out between the lines of slow-moving ships.

<You can't leave,> I told myself. <There's still Rachel and Marco and Tobias and Ax.>

But going back meant facing the fact that there were no longer six of us. Going back meant admitting that Jake was gone.

Then, suddenly, I was lying on cobblestones, dry.

Of course. What a fool I was. I couldn't escape. I was still tied to the Time Matrix. And now I'd been yanked along again, helpless, unable to resist, unable to escape.

Maybe I could just lie there. A dolphin lying in an alley in some place, some time, probably some new pointless war . . . I didn't want to be human again. I wanted to stay inside that dolphin brain.

But, of course, that wasn't happening, was it? The dolphin was no longer happy. The dolphin's instincts were sending panic signals.

Beached! No water! Helpless!

I began to demorph.

Someone stood over me, knelt beside me.

"Come on, pick it up, morph!" Tobias said. "People are coming!"

Too late. My left eye spotted a group of people coming down the alleyway, leather-soled shoes loud on the uneven stones. Three guys, maybe nineteen, maybe twenty years old.

<Where are we?> I asked.

"Princeton University. Don't ask me why."

<The others?>

"Not yet," Tobias said. "Not that I've seen, anyway. I don't know . . . Marco and Ax were with me, right at the end. Maybe they made it. I don't know. But Rachel . . . Rachel, she . . ."

He didn't have to say it.

<No, no, no,> I moaned.

"It didn't end with Jake," Tobias said. "We all . . . Look, we have to end this. We have to take this guy down. So demorph, we have work to do."

My beak melted away, the teeth turning watery, then rehardened, forming my own teeth.

I did it all on automatic. Rachel! I should have been there for her. I had run away, nursing my wounds. I'd abandoned Rachel when she needed me.

"What is that thing?" It was a southern accent. He began trotting toward us.

"It's a dolphin turning into a girl," Tobias said. "I'd explain but trust me, you wouldn't understand."

"My God!" another student, short and dark-haired, gasped. "We must send for a doctor at once!"

His eyes were wide with horror. I couldn't blame him. I was a writhing mass of rubbery flesh and shifting bones. Legs were growing from a dolphin tail, arms from flippers.

"Just keep demorphing," Tobias told me. "We have to get after Visser Four. Forget security, we don't have time to worry about it. Hey! Any of you guys know what year this is?"

"Why, it's a colored girl!" the third guy said. He looked down at me with concerned blue eyes.

"I've never seen the like of this!"

"Hey, guys, help us out, okay? What year? What country?"

"Don't answer him, he could be a spy!"

I was almost entirely human. I stood up, shaky. "Sorry," I said. "I know it's kind of gross to watch."

"How did you do that?" the man with the southern accent demanded. And then, like some vile punctuation, he added a word I won't repeat.

CHAPTER 29
Cassie

It was like a slap. I couldn't answer. I just gaped.

"What did you call her?" Tobias asked.

The student shoved Tobias hard against his chest and sent him sprawling back. "I'm not addressing you, little boy; I'm talking to this creature, here." He grabbed me by the shoulder and shook me. "Speak up when a white man asks you a question."

"Hey, this isn't Alabama, Davis," the short student protested.

Davis ignored him. "Don't tell me how to deal with coloreds, Friedman. Most likely this is some kind of runaway slave."

I shot a glance at Tobias. In his human morph

he could do little. And he'd have to pass through his hawk form before getting to what Marco would call "serious firepower."

But that was okay. This small battle was all mine. I didn't want any help.

"You don't like black people, Mr. Davis?" I said pleasantly. "No problem. I can turn white. Watch me."

Most of the time I'd probably have let it go. I'd been called names before. I'd run into racism before. Mostly I figured people like that were just sad, weak-minded fools. So most of the time I just avoided people like that.

But I had been in three wars since breakfast. I had seen Jake shot down. I'd just learned that Rachel, my best friend, was gone.

I was sad and ashamed and filled with rage, all at once. So this wasn't "most of the time."

White fur began to grow from my face. Actually, it was clear fur, hollow needles of fur that were designed to keep the polar bear warm. But the fur looked white, taken altogether.

My hands swelled, big as dinner plates. Long, raked claws extended from the fingertips.

I was growing whiter. And bigger. Much, much bigger.

"It's some kind of voodoo trick!" Davis wailed.

Tobias was back on his feet, arms crossed over his chest, looking on calmly. "You two guys may want to step back out of the way because I don't think Davis here is going to be having a very good day."

I loomed larger and larger.

Davis began to back away, pressing against one alley wall. But sheer amazement and disbelief kept him from running until it was too late.

Finally, he broke and ran. I slammed a pile-driver front leg into the wall and blocked his way.

<Don't you like me?> I asked.

He turned the other way. I slammed my other front leg to block his escape.

"Nah, nah, don't kill me! Don't kill me!" He looked at Tobias. "Don't let her kill me."

Tobias shrugged.

With a sudden movement I opened my jaws, twisted my head sideways, and clamped my mouth over the guy's face.

"HhhhhRROOOAARRR!"

Davis's cheeks vibrated from the sound waves. His hair blew back.

"Personally, I'd apologize if I were you," Tobias suggested.

Davis babbled his apology into my open mouth. He kept apologizing even after I let him sink to the ground.

"Whoa, Cassie! That is *so* Rachel," Marco said. I recognized the voice immediately. He'd come up behind us.

And that was surprising enough. But then . . .

"Really," Rachel said. "What are you doing? Stealing my act?"

"Rachel!" Tobias yelped. And a millisecond later he had spun around, grabbed her, and kissed her. Then he held her back at arm's length. "You're dead!"

<Rachel! You're dead,> I agreed.

"No, I'm not," Rachel said.

"Yes, you are. I saw it!" Tobias cried.

"I am seriously *not* dead."

<I am convinced that she is not dead,> Ax said. He was in full Andalite form, wildly out of place in a cobblestoned alley on a leafy campus.

Blue Eyes let out a moan. "What are you people? You're not human!"

<You are correct. I am an Andalite,> Ax said.

"Let's focus," Marco interrupted. "Rachel remembers morphing to chimpanzee. She remembers climbing into the rigging. Then, nothing. Suddenly she's here, and so am I, and by the way, not that I'm complaining because at least no one is shooting, but where *is* here?"

"Princeton University," Tobias said.

"Say what? Why?"

"Good question. Now, we want some answers," Tobias said, addressing Friedman and the boy with sympathetic blue eyes. "Let's start with the basics: What year is this?"

CHAPTER 30
Tobias

"It's nineteen thirty-four," Blue Eyes said. Then added, "sir."

I looked at the others, perplexed. I shook my head. 1934? Princeton University? Why?

<Is anything happening here? Anything unusual?> Cassie asked the students. <I mean, aside from me and him?>

They shook their heads.

"Something weird about all this," I said. "It's Agincourt, a war, Washington crossing the Delaware, a war, Trafalgar, a war, then this?"

"What's Trafalgar?" Marco asked.

The students must have thought he was asking them. "It's a naval battle between Britain and

France. The British lost, the French won. It led to us having to make peace with Napoleon."

Cassie looked at me again, like I'd understand. I shrugged. "I don't know, it's a mess. Whatever was supposed to happen at Agincourt, I think it happened. We saved the king and all. But Washington wasn't supposed to die, and he did. And I think maybe the English were supposed to win, but didn't. So . . . so I don't know!"

<I may have an idea,> Cassie said. <Maybe Visser Four has outsmarted himself. He's here expecting something, right? But maybe whatever it was supposed to be has been altered by what he's already done. He changed the past so whatever was supposed to happen here and now isn't happening.>

"My head is going to explode," Marco said. "You need to be Einstein to figure this —"

"Einstein?" Friedman interrupted. "Do you mean Albert Einstein, the German physicist?"

"Yeah. Albert Einstein. Like there's another?" Marco said.

"But he's in Germany."

"You know," Blue Eyes interrupted, "there was a crazy fellow over in the Dean's office yelling about Einstein. He was dressed very oddly, like a sailor, perhaps. I thought at first he was a member of the philosophy faculty, but —"

"Big slash up the side of his face?"

"Why, yes."

Marco snapped his fingers. "That's it. Visser Four came here to kill Einstein!"

"But he's not here," Rachel said.

"Exactly. But he was *supposed* to be. Visser Four didn't realize he'd already changed this time line. Something that happened at Agincourt or the Delaware or Trafalgar screwed this up."

"Dude," I snapped at Friedman. "What does 'e' equal?"

"What?"

"'E' equals . . ."

"By 'e' you mean energy?" Friedman said.

<They don't know,> Cassie said. <They don't know that "e" equals "mc" squared.>

"Maybe Einstein doesn't know it, either."

<No "e" equals "mc" squared, no atomic bomb.>

"Yeah. The question is: Is that a good thing, or a bad thing?"

CHAPTER 31
Marco

Cassie let Davis crawl away. We let the other two guys go, too.

We weren't too worried about what they might do. We figured we wouldn't be at Princeton University for long anyway. What were they going to do, arrest us? We'd had people after us with swords, lances, arrows, muskets, and cannons. Campus cops were not a major worry.

"Look, Visser Four has already figured out Einstein isn't here," Rachel said. "He's going to jump again. Maybe already has. We need a plan. Fast."

"Or at least a clue," Cassie muttered. She was back in her usual form. She looked strangely at Rachel. "Tobias saw you blown in half, Rachel.

Why are you back? Why are you alive? And why isn't . . . why *isn't* Jake?"

"I don't know," Rachel admitted.

<The Drode said Crayak had demanded a life in payment,> Ax pointed out. <The terms were negotiated between Crayak and the Ellimist. Perhaps the Ellimist had his own demands: That it be *only* one life.>

Tobias said, "Wait a minute. You mean . . . you mean the rest of us *can't* die?"

<I am speculating. I would not wish to test my theory.>

"Yeah, guess not," Cassie agreed.

Rachel slammed her fist into her palm. "We have to get Visser Four. That's the bottom line, here."

"Agreed," Tobias said. "Visser Four is meat."

"No."

Everyone stared at me.

"No," I repeated. "We're missing the point. It's not about Visser Four. It's the Time Matrix. Look, Washington has already died, the English have already lost at whatever, Einstein . . . I don't know, but he's not where he's supposed to be, doing what he's supposed to be doing."

"So we still have to hammer Visser Four."

"No. No. Don't you guys get it? It's not enough to take him down. We need the Time Matrix ourselves. Because Washington *has* to cross the

Delaware. And Admiral Nelson probably has to beat the French. And Einstein has to come to Princeton. We can't just stop Visser Four. We have to go back and rewrite history."

They were all staring at me again. Cassie's mouth was open. Rachel was beginning a slow grin.

I got frustrated. "Don't you guys get it? We have to get the stupid Matrix and go back and — Oh . . . my . . . God!" It hit me then. What had already hit the others.

"Jake," Cassie said.

Ax looked doubtful. <Crayak demanded a death.>

"He got a death," Tobias said. "Jake died. Is there a law that says he has to *stay* that way?"

I intercepted Cassie's gaze and then we both looked away. We'd been naive, stupid. We'd thought we could save him, that we could stop death from finding him. We hadn't even been able to shout a warning.

There was a noise at the end of the alleyway. Two police officers were sauntering up, looking bored until they spotted Ax.

They drew their guns.

"N-n-no one move!"

"It's okay, officers, there's nothing to —"

Suddenly, I was at the mall. People were running. I heard someone babble, "It just appeared, this big round ball thing! Right in front of —"

Then, just as suddenly, I was standing on an open, empty desert plain at twilight or sunrise, it was impossible to tell.

"What the . . ."

I saw Rachel pop into view. She was as confused as me. Then Ax.

Instantly I was standing at the bottom of a hill, people pressed all around me. Some were wearing togas.

Not frat-party, let's-drink-beer togas. The original togas.

And the building at the top of the hill had tall white columns I'd seen before. What was it called? The . . . Colosseum? No.

<The Parthenon!> Tobias exclaimed, swooping down low over my head.

"What's going on?" I yelled up at him.

<Visser Four,> Ax said, suddenly standing not five feet away and causing a near riot among the Greeks. <He is attempting to extend the diffusion effect.>

"You mean he's trying to lose us?"

<Precisely. He's jumping rapidly, time to time, hoping to delay us. Evidently what he plans next requires —>

I was on a grassy slope. It was hot.

It was going to get a lot hotter because up the slope I saw men behind barricades of dirt and logs and bales of hay. Long gun barrels were poking out from behind the barricade.

Down the slope was an army dressed in gray. They also carried guns and brandished swords and held big flags aloft. And they were walking resolutely up the hill.

"Ooooookay, let's just time shift again," I muttered. "Let's just not stay here. Let's just go somewhere —"

A splash of icy water hit my face. I tasted salt. I was lurching, wallowing, in a boat again. But smaller, open. Steel. Gray steel beside me, an open-topped gray box.

Men pressed in around me. They wore dark green. Helmets were pulled low on furrowed brows. Shoulders hunched, flinching, faces scared white, teeth bared, eyes staring forward.

Ba-WHUMPF!

An explosion drenched me with spray. It rocked the boat like a hammer blow.

"Who the heck are *you*?" a sergeant demanded.

CHAPTER 32
Marco

"Where are we?" I asked, chattering out the words. The fear was contagious.

Ba-WHUMPF! Ba-WHUMPF!

Explosions all around.

"You some kind of stowaway, kid?" the sergeant said, laughing humorlessly. "Picked one rotten place to catch a joyride."

"Yeah, well, I don't know if I'm staying or not. Where are we?" I asked again.

"We're in the English Channel, son, but we are about to be in France. Normandy."

Normandy. Even I knew what that meant. I'd seen the movies.

D-Day. World War II. The invasion of Europe

by American and British forces. Only, there was no such place as "America."

"Oh, no," I whispered.

The sergeant laughed. "Yeah: 'Oh, no!' Here we go, ladies. Keep your heads down and your weapons high and dry."

Scrrrunch!

The boat jarred to a stop.

The ramp dropped.

RAT-TAT-TAT-TAT-TAT-TAT-TAT!

The sergeant fell with two holes through his chest. Men were dropping all around me. It was the Delaware all over again, only now the death was faster.

I caught a brief glimpse of sandy beach. Men lying prone, alive or dead, who could tell. A bluff topped with barbed wire and a low, menacing concrete bunker.

I dropped on my butt, spun around, and hugged the floor. Men fell back on me. I began to morph.

RAT-TAT-TAT-TAT-TAT-TAT!

I didn't have a morph strong enough for this. This was massacre by machine gun. I needed to get small. Too small for the bullets to find me.

I was going fly, and I was going there fast.

Men were bleeding on me. I was screaming. I didn't care anymore. I was just getting out of there alive.

I shrank. The bodies sagged down on top of me.

RAT-TAT-TAT-TAT-TAT-TAT!

Machine-gun bullets continued pouring into the mass over me. Those that were still alive wouldn't be for long. And I'd have been dead myself, but for the protection of men whose flesh protected mine.

I shrank. My bones crunched and shriveled and finally turned watery and disappeared.

My eyes bulged huge, faceted, glittering, then shrank along with the rest of me.

Legs sprouted from my chest. My own arms and legs became elongated, jointed sticks. Dagger-sharp hairs stuck out along their length.

But I wasn't noticing much of that. I was noticing the fact that my brain was about to explode. Too much death and destruction and horror. As bad as my life had been at times as an Animorph, I'd seen real hard-core combat now and it was worse. The men who died in these battles had been like Jake: They'd had no chance.

Here, at Agincourt, back on the Delaware River, or on the beautiful, slow-moving sailing ship. No difference.

Men stood up in the face of the enemy and were massacred. Arrows found throats. Swords found vulnerable flesh. Cannons ripped away limbs. Bullets entered organs by neat, round holes and came out in a shredded mess. Men died never having the chance to resist, to fight, to run, to cry out, to prepare, to wonder.

One second they were scared and brave and alive. The next second they were dead.

Just like Jake.

Cassie and I had sworn to protect him. But there'd never even been a chance.

I shrank and morphed, less and less human. Gossamer wings sprouted from my back. My face, my tongue and mouth and teeth all merged, melted together, extended out into a hollow tube through which I would dribble saliva and suck up liquid food.

My fly eyes saw a world of shattered images, faceted, a broken mirror. Broken mirrors filled with huge limbs arrayed like a cage around me.

I fired my wings and rose up through the maze of arms and legs and heads, out into the air.

Explosions rocked me. But they did not touch me. The bullets would not find me except by the most amazingly long odds. Yet the air was so thick with flying lead that I still felt fear.

Up, out of the boat, which now drifted helplessly, its coxswain dead along with every other man who'd tried to come ashore.

The fly's vision was not good at a distance. I could see only what was close. And then, not in detail.

I was glad. I didn't want to see what was around me.

But I could not block the fly's sense of smell. I smelled, tasted the spilled blood and drained bodily fluids. I couldn't help but smell them.

D-Day. The smell alone would haunt me for the rest of my life.

CHAPTER 33

Ax

I time-jumped into water. My hooves absorbed some of it. It had a high salt content. I kicked wildly, looking for bottom. My hooves touched sand. I propelled myself through the surf, onto a sandy beach.

Ka-WHUMPF!

I flew through the air. I saw a gray sky overhead. I saw humans around me, running, lying down, falling. I hit the sand hard.

I lay there, breath knocked out of me.

My main eyes were staring upward. At the sky. The blue atmosphere of Earth, beyond which was the black of space, the now-invisible points of stars, the disappearingly small planets.

One of which, somewhere up there, far, far away, was my own.

I had never wanted to be there more.

I thought I understood humans. I understood nothing.

They were mad! Lunatics. Evil, violent, destructive, hate-filled creatures.

<Ax-man! Are you hit?>

It was Tobias. I saw him, drifting, wings spread wide, above the smoke of battle.

<I am not injured,> I said. <But I must tell you: I am profoundly tired of your people.>

<I'm not exactly thrilled with them myself,> Tobias said. <But you need to morph, man. Nothing on that beach is getting out alive. I just talked to Marco, he's in fly morph. Not a bad idea to get wings.>

Chnth-chnth-chnth!

Bullets hit the sand beside my head. I scooted sideways just as another burst tore up the sand where my head had been.

I began to morph. Tobias and Marco were both right: Wings. I was sprouting harrier feathers as the next explosion hit the beach near me and pelted me with sand.

<Anyone else here?> It was Cassie's voice.

<Yes, I am here. So are Marco and Tobias,> I answered. <Are you safe?>

<As safe as anyone could be,> she said. <I materialized right at the bottom of the bluff, in some bushes. I morphed to osprey. I'm in the air, now.>

I was nearly done morphing. I had wings and talons. My front legs were tiny, shrunken appendages. My stalk eyes were gone. My main eyes had begun to acquire the piercing hawk intensity.

My face was a perfect melding of Andalite and harrier. Gray feathers and blue fur. An opening had appeared in my lower face, the beginnings of a mouth, a beak.

Ka-WHUMPF!

Dirt buried me. Blackness all around me. In panic I kicked with tiny talons and shriveled front legs. But the wet sand clung to me, refusing to be shoved aside.

Demorph! I knew I had to demorph. No other way to —

Ka-WHUMPF!

Something landed on me. Crushing weight. But the sand was off my face. I saw daylight. I pushed and shoved and wiggled my way, with a body that was almost useless.

I began to demorph, the panic under better control now that I had at least a glimpse of sky.

"I'm hit! I'm hit! Medic!"

The voice was shockingly close. Only then did

I realize what had landed on me, pinning me down under the sand.

A human was lying on me, unaware. He struggled up, lessening the weight on me.

"No, nononono!" he moaned and fell back.

I had to get out from under him. Had to get away. All I had to do was get off the ground, reach the sky. Had to demorph to Andalite first, push my way clear.

But the human was moaning. He was crying. He was calling for his mother.

Not my affair. The madness of humans was not my concern.

Another human slammed into the sand beside me. "I'm here, buddy," this human said.

My stalk eyes grew from the bird head. I pushed one up and out of the sand. I saw the injured human. I am not an expert on human physiology, but I believed the wound to be fatal.

The second human was tending to him. He ripped feverishly at the wounded soldier's clothing. He jabbed a syringe into the man's arm.

"Doc. Doc. Is it bad? It hurts. It hurts. Ohhhhh!"

"You'll be fine, soldier. Morphine will —"

Chnth-chnth-chnth!

Bullets ripped the sand. The "Doc" flinched. He resettled his helmet on his head. He did not leave.

BOOOM!

An explosion, not twenty feet away showered us again with sand.

"Don't let me die, don't let me die."

"You'll be okay, soldier. I'm just gonna —"

The "Doc" fell atop the wounded man. A bullet had penetrated his throat. Dead. While trying to save a man he must have known was doomed.

Was this Visser Four's doing? Or was this all simply a part of human history? I felt a desperate need to think, to make sense of it all.

One thing I knew: The battle on the river had not been part of human history. My friends were sure of that. At that point Visser Four had twisted the strands of history.

The sea battle? No one seemed to know how that was supposed to have happened. Had the battle even taken place originally?

One thing was certain: Visser Four had miscalculated at the university. Things were not as he'd expected them to be. And if we were now even later in time, this battle, too, might not be all he'd expected.

Visser Four might be as confused as we were.

And yet, in the end, as we'd seen, Visser Four had altered history to create an Earth of harsh repression.

But then was then, that was "before" we had

become involved. Before this new version of history where we'd stymied Visser Four at Agincourt.

What did it all mean? What was I missing? Surely there was a way to make sense of it all, to encapsulate all this mindless killing, all this violence, all this fear in a package of reason, logic . . .

I was afraid. The realization surprised me. I was hiding beneath two dead bodies, spinning the wheels of my mind trying to make sense of things.

Thinking was so much easier than sliding out from beneath this grizzly protection and facing the murder all around me.

I was a coward!

No, this was not my war. My war was with the Yeerks. This was human killing human in some dark, distant past. Insanity! Lunacy!

Coward!

No! I had no chance. Everyone on that beach was dying. Everyone was going to die. Everyone! This wasn't my beach. This wasn't my war. Not my place to die.

Not my place to kill. As I had killed the Hessian officer.

<Marco! Rachel! Ax!> It was Cassie's thought-speak voice. Faint. Far away.

Don't answer, I told myself. *Hide! Don't answer!*

<Visser Four! Tobias and I see him. He's in a jeep, leading a column of tanks! We need help.>

Not my war, I said again.

Then I began to morph and push the sand away.

CHAPTER 34

Cassie

It moved beneath me, a sinister gray snake, clanking and lurching and belching sudden gusts of black diesel smoke.

The tank column approached the beach along a narrow, winding road. At the head of the column, an open, jeep-style car pulling a trailer.

In the trailer was a glowing, golden ball as tall as a man. A weapon far more powerful than all the tanks of all the armies of the world combined.

The Time Matrix.

The Time Matrix had allowed Visser Four to reach the German tanks and tell their generals that this was the real invasion. That this was the time to strike the allies.

In the passenger seat of the jeep, sitting with three machine-gun–toting German soldiers behind him, was Visser Four.

There was a bloody cut down one side of his face, barely concealed by hastily applied bandages.

The tank column extended as far as I could see down the road. More tanks had pulled off into fields defined by tall, impenetrable hedges.

Directly beneath me was the bluff overlooking the beach. It bristled with concrete bunkers and trenches and barbed wire. Dozens of machine guns, cannon, mortars, all aimed down at the vulnerable men on the beach below.

Beyond the bloody beach a huge, gray fleet kept station and lobbed shells that missed the bunkers and exploded harmlessly in the fields behind.

In ten minutes the first tanks would reach the bluff above the beach. And then, all hope of an Allied victory would die. The Germans would win. And the world would be the world we had glimpsed briefly.

<We need everyone!> I yelled, flapping my wings to regain lost altitude.

Tobias drifted close to me. <If no one else gets here it's going to be up to us.>

<What are we supposed to do? All those Germans in all those tanks aren't just going to let us

attack Visser Four and steal the Time Matrix. Besides, do you know how to operate the stupid Time Matrix?>

<Me? I can't program a speed-dial,> Tobias admitted. <But those tanks cannot reach that beach. This is D-Day, and if the Germans win, the Americans and the English lose the biggest war in history!>

<But there are no Americans,> I said.

<Whatever they're called, what does it matter? This is D-Day! This is Normandy. This decides whether the Nazis go on or are stopped.>

<Where are the others?> I demanded. Not that I had any right. Where had I been at Trafalgar? Hiding. Escaping.

<We can't do this as birds,> Tobias said.

<No. I know. The road curves past that last stand of trees down there. That's the place.>

<We'll have to hurry,> Tobias said. He spilled air from his wings and glided toward the trees below us. I turned and followed him down.

We landed amid blasted trunks. Artillery had blown away all but a few desperate, spring-green leaves.

<What do you think the Nazis will make of a Hork-Bajir?> Tobias wondered. He began morphing as soon as he landed. Hork-Bajir horns sprouted from his forehead.

I focused on the wolf DNA inside me. The

wolf was fast, strong. No match for machine guns.

I might reach Visser Four before I was gunned down. I might not. Either way I wouldn't survive.

Unless, of course, Ax was right and only Jake could be killed.

I felt sick.

<Thinking about how Rachel came back?> Tobias asked.

<Yeah.>

<Me, too.>

<Doesn't exactly make it easier, does it?>

"No," I said as I finished demorphing to human. I began immediately morphing the wolf. I could hear the clank-clank-clank of tank treads. I could hear the roar of their engines.

The Germans. The Nazis. The ultimate evil.

Worth dying to stop them. Yes. Worth my one, puny life.

But I didn't want to die. No matter how great the cause. No matter the reason.

<Ready?> Tobias asked. He was fully Hork-Bajir.

I sniffed the breeze. My wolf's nose told me stories of things far beyond this battle. It told me of cows and calves grazing peacefully in their fields. Chickens. Foxes. Rats. Sheep.

This was farm country. Not much different from my own farm, probably. But my nose also smelled cordite, charred wood, diesel exhaust, and blood.

I could hear too much, too well. I heard the tank engines, the tank gears grinding, the treads as they slapped the mud. I heard the explosions, large and small. The cries, distant but piercing.

<Maybe if we get the Time Matrix . . . maybe we can do more than just put it all back together, you know?>

<What do you mean?>

<I mean history is nothing but killing. Maybe we could change that.>

<Let's just go get Visser Four,> Tobias said. <For Jake.>

<For Jake,> I said.

The words were out before I thought about them. For Jake. Revenge. Kill the killer. Avenge the wrong.

And I was going to rewrite history?

The jeep was close now. I could see it clearly through the trees. And I could see Visser Four.

I could also see the machine guns gripped tightly.

<Now,> Tobias said softly.

We began to run.

Fast! Faster! Stunted, ruined trees zipped by. We hurtled over scraggly bushes. The wind was in my face, the wind of my own speed. Tobias, Hork-Bajir, was running beside me, blades flashing.

I saw the Visser. I saw the Time Matrix. I saw the lead tank with its insignia emblazoned on the side.

I leaped!

Wrong!

Too late!

I was already flying, my bone-crunching jaws already open, ready for the enemy's throat.

"*Mon dieu!*" the French soldier yelled.

BapBapBapBapBapBapBapBap!

Tobias tripped and went down. A line of bullet holes painted red circles across his chest.

I hit Visser Four and closed my jaw over his arm. We tumbled out of the jeep, onto the ground. Only then did I see the handcuffs that held the Visser's wrists.

CHAPTER 35

Ax

I had joined with Marco and Rachel. We had taken to the air. We were still far away when we saw Tobias and Cassie morphing in the woods.

My harrier eyes spotted them easily. But not till after I'd spotted the Time Matrix.

It was an awesome thing to contemplate. It would not make an Andalite or a human the equal of the Ellimist in power, but it represented far more destructive power than the combined fleets of the Andalite people and the Yeerk empire.

I wondered how it had come to Earth. And I wondered how my brother, Elfangor, had known it was on Earth. Because surely he had known. Visser Four was right: Elfangor had chosen the spot deliberately. It was no coincidence that he had landed, had died, within a few feet of this machine.

Perhaps, if we survived, I could ask the Ellimist for an explanation. As certain as I was that Elfangor was involved, I was certain that the Ellimist was, too.

All of this was tied to Elfangor's earlier sojourn on Earth. The lost time that had resulted in the birth of his son, Tobias. All of it led here.

<There it is,> Rachel said. <And there *he* is: Visser Four.>

<D-Day, man,> Marco said. He sounded shaken. I don't know what he had encountered on that beach, but I could guess that it was not far different than what I had found there.

I was still trembling from the fear. From the fear of my own fear. From images I would never be able to wash from my mind.

We flew to intercept Cassie and Tobias. The breeze was with us. It would not take long. But would we be able to intercept Visser Four and stop his intervention? That was the question.

<I take it, Marco, that you are familiar with this war,> I said.

<This is the big one of all big ones,> Marco said. <World War Two. The Nazis try and take over the world and almost do it. The Japanese at-

tack Pearl Harbor. D-Day, Battle of the Bulge, John Wayne at Iwo Jima.>

<And the Holocaust,> Rachel said.

<Holocaust?>

<The Germans, the Nazis under Hitler, murdered six million Jews — men, women, and children.>

Obviously Rachel had misspoken. <These Jews were an opposing army?>

<No. Jews are a religion, or a race, I guess. My dad's Jewish. Mostly the Jews in the Holocaust were Germans and Poles. You know, civilians. Normal people. Others, too: Gypsies, gays, handicapped people. They were taken to camps and shot or starved or killed with poison gas. Children killed in their mothers' arms.>

She spoke with no special emphasis. No anger.

Human emotion is often confusing, in part because each individual human expresses it differently. Rachel is quick to anger over small things. The larger things render her cold and seemingly emotionless.

But then what emotion could possibly be sufficiently intense to encompass the crimes she described?

Humans. I wondered, not for the first time, but now with renewed intensity, whether the

Yeerks had any notion of the species they proposed to conquer. Humans seemed to exist across too broad a spectrum to even be considered a single species.

The same species that spawned my friends, Jake, Cassie, Marco, Rachel, my *shorm* and "nephew" Tobias, seemed to revel in mutual slaughter and sank to depths no Yeerk would sink to. Depths of depraved brutality that would be unimaginable to an Andalite.

<Even humans —> I began. I stopped myself. I should not insult humans. This was not the time or the place. We were racing to intercept the Yeerk, to save the future, to . . . But my mind was boiling. Too much!

That human warrior would stand against human warrior and kill, that was wrong and foolish and stupid. But that humans, the species I was risking my own life to help, were capable of such a filthy, cowardly thing as the deliberate slaughter of innocents . . .

Not at all like the things I had done in combat. Not at all like fighting Hork-Bajir-Controllers, or Taxxons or . . . or Hessian officers.

I jerked my thoughts away from that memory. From the memory of my tail blade snapping forward.

<We Andalites have fought wars among ourselves in the past. We did not kill children. It is

not possible to conceive of a greater evil than the deliberate killing of a child.>

<Yeah, well, we do know that, Ax,> Marco said resentfully. <Why do you think those guys down on the beach are dying?>

<Those tanks coming down that road? Those are Nazi tanks,> Rachel said. <So let's stop them.>

<We are after the Time Matrix,> Marco reminded her.

<Maybe you are. You and Ax go get the Time Matrix. I'm getting a Nazi.>

CHAPTER 36

Cassie

I rolled over. The Visser cried out in pain. He tried to get up, but he couldn't use his hands; they were held together by the handcuffs.

Tobias lay bleeding.

<Tobias! Demorph!>

But then, to my amazement, he simply sat up. The bullet holes in his chest were gone!

<It's true,> he whispered, touching his chest with a Hork-Bajir claw. <Just Jake. The rest of us . . . we can't be killed.>

BANG! BANG! BANG! BANG!

I felt the bullets hit me. Neck. Head. Shoulder. Head.

I felt the impact, power blows. I felt sharp, overwhelming pain. And then . . .

I was still alive.

The tank column rolled by. Infantrymen rushed up alongside the tanks to surround us. They waved guns at a wolf and a monster, scared of both, unsure what to do.

Visser Four tried to crawl away but one of the soldiers gave him a kick in the stomach that dropped the Controller on his face.

An officer pulled his pistol from a holster, walked cautiously up to me, held the barrel against my head, and . . .

BLAM! BLAM!

I fell over.

I stood up.

"*C'est pas possible!*" the officer gasped in French.

"*Es ist ein wolfman,*" one of the soldiers said in German.

French and Germans together. Not Germans alone.

I looked at the insignia on the epaulet of the officer. It was a shield, slashed down the middle at an angle, half of it the French tricolor, blue, white, and red, the other half a stylized black eagle.

<What is going on?> Tobias wondered, as confused as I was. <This isn't the way it was! This isn't right!>

The soldiers, the French and German soldiers, kept their guns trained on us. They were confused and afraid.

I could identify.

I looked at the soldiers. They were a mix of old men and young kids, some who looked no more than fifteen. Some of the older ones could have been my grandfather.

The French officer said something about "*le capitaine.*" The captain. The Germans agreed with whatever he'd said. I think he'd said they should all wait for the captain to get there.

Several of the soldiers broke out cigarettes. Some drank from their canteens. The tanks rolled slowly by.

Visser Four raised himself to a sitting position. The jeep hauling the Time Matrix had pulled off the road. He was edging, ever so slowly . . .

<Don't let him reach that thing,> Tobias said in thought-speak.

The French officer understood immediately. He jerked his head and two of his men dragged the Controller back to where we sat in our weird little standoff.

"I just want to know one thing, Andalites: How did you follow me? I have the Time Matrix! How did you follow me? And why, why, *why* don't you die?"

<Visser Three's been trying to kill us for some time, now,> Tobias said. <We're hard to kill.>

The Controller made a face of hatred and resentment. "I should have used the Time Matrix to destroy Visser Three. That bungling fool!"

<We'd have helped you,> Tobias said with a laugh. Then, privately, to me, he said, <Cassie, if we can't be killed, we don't need to worry about these soldiers. We can take the Time Matrix right now.>

<Yeah. I . . . I guess that's true. But, I don't know, it's weird. I mean, I guess we are sort of immortal for now, but who knows? A gun is still a gun. Are you a hundred-percent sure?>

Tobias made a Hork-Bajir smile. <Ninety-nine percent. The remaining one percent says if we push it we're toast.>

Suddenly another jeep-type car came rumbling up along the line of tanks. An officer, a German, jumped out and trotted over to us.

In a mix of French and German the soldiers and their officer explained this exceedingly unusual situation. The captain was a middle-aged man with a lined, scarred face and tired eyes. He obviously knew about the big, glowing globe. He seemed to know, too, about the prisoner, Visser Four.

But seeing a Hork-Bajir sitting there beside a seemingly tame — and unkillable — wolf was new. He leaned close to Tobias and gingerly touched his wrist blade.

<I won't hurt you,> Tobias said.

The captain answered in German. Then tried French. Finally, excellent English. "Do you understand English?"

<Yes, we do,> I said.

He snapped his head around. There was a quick burst of German including a word that sounded like "wolf" and another that was very recognizable: "Frankenstein."

<He thinks you're a monster, Tobias.>

Then, in English once more, he said, "I do not know how a monster and a talking wolf come to be here. Explain."

I started to answer. Not to explain, because explaining would have been utterly impossible. Or at least it would have taken a solid week.

But then, I saw the old man who'd been driving the captain's jeep climb down from behind the wheel. He was in his fifties, at least, although his uniform indicated a low rank. He was stocky, not very tall. His black hair was parted high on his head. His eyes were dark and intense. He wore a small mustache.

A style of mustache known everywhere as a Hitler mustache.

CHAPTER 37
Rachel

Far below us, Tobias and Cassie seemed to be chatting with Nazi soldiers guarding Visser Four. They were problem number two, as far as I was concerned.

Problem number one? The tanks that were rolling toward the beach. Huge, clanking monsters armored to withstand a direct hit from a cannon.

I have several powerful morphs. But none that would so much as annoy a tank.

However, the tank hatches were open. Their officers or drivers or whatever stood with heads and shoulders visible. No one was shooting at them. They had not reached the battle.

When they did, the invasion of Normandy would end in utter defeat for the invaders.

<We have to stop them,> I said.

Marco snorted angrily. <How? Morph to elephant and go one-on-one with a tank and you'll end up roadkill.>

<Our morphing ability is a potent weapon, Rachel, but useless here,> Ax said.

<We're stopping them,> I said flatly. <That road is narrow. It's cut deep. Kill one tank and the others will have a hard time going around it. At least we'd slow them down.>

<Yeah, then one of us gets to the ships offshore and directs them where to fire,> Marco said. <Great in theory. Just one problem: How do a bunch of birds kill a tank?>

<I don't know, all right?> I admitted. <I just know we have to!>

<I may have an idea,> Ax said. <I have been observing your primitive human weapons. Several are fascinating. Most could be very easily improved upon, and —>

<Get to the point!> I yelled.

<The small, hand-held explosive devices. They are roughly spherical in shape with a ludicrously crude priming device. They are thrown and —>

Marco said, <Hand grenades?>

<They are very weak explosives,> Ax said.

<However, within the confined space of a tank's interior they could —>

<If I had lips and you had a mouth I'd kiss you!> I said. <Hand grenades! That's it! We'll drop hand grenades down the hatch of the lead tank.>

<How do we carry one? How do we pull the pin?> Marco demanded.

I laughed. <Details, Marco. Minor details. Let's find some grenades.>

We flew back over the bluff. I wasn't going down to the beach if I could avoid it. The bodies down there were so thick on the ground that in some places we could have stepped from body to body without ever touching the sand.

Fire was still pouring down from the protected positions on the bluff. Landing craft were still disgorging men. It was a second wave, I suppose. A whole new assault, adding new victims. Like cattle going down the chute to the slaughtering floor.

But, of course, cattle don't know what's coming. Humans do. They saw the bodies of their fellow soldiers. They heard the explosions. They smelled the death. And they still came.

War is obscene, the worst thing humans do. But warriors, the individual men, are the very best of humanity. Not because they are willing to kill. But because they are willing to risk death, to sacrifice themselves for others.

I was high in the air, not safe, but so, so much safer. I felt like a coward.

<Over here!> Marco said. <They're issuing grenades to some guys down at the base of the bluff. There's an open case of them.>

<Okay. I'm biggest,> I said. <I'll do it.>

<Are you confident that you can carry the weight?> Ax asked.

<I don't know. Bald eagles snatch whole salmon out of the water. How much can a hand grenade weigh?>

<How much does a salmon weigh?> Marco answered rhetorically.

I floated on a high breeze coming off the water. My wings were filled by warm June thermals. I wondered if the warm updrafts were strengthened by the heat of red-hot gun barrels.

A dozen guys were huddled together at the base of the bluff. Americans. Or at least, I reminded myself, they should have been Americans.

They looked lost and scared and exhausted. Their sergeant had a steel ammunition box open between his knees. He was handing out grenades, two at a time.

It would take speed and precision. And a distraction.

<Marco? Ax? I need that guy to look away.>

<Yeah. We're on it.>

Marco and Ax, an osprey and a harrier, formed up beside me. We'd have looked weird and out of place. If anyone had had time to bird-watch.

<Now!>

Ax and Marco spilled air, narrowed their tails, and plunged.

Down, down, down!

I went after them, twenty feet behind. I could feel the air turbulence from their wings.

No problem, I told myself. Marco and Ax swoop close, the sergeant looks away, I snatch the grenades out of his hand, and —

CRUMPF!

The mortar shell landed in the middle of the men.

The shock wave knocked Ax and Marco down like they were flies hit by a giant swatter.

CHAPTER 38

Cassie

<Is that . . .>

<Yeah. I think so,> I said.

<Oh, my God.>

<A long way from God,> I muttered.

Adolf Hitler. The most evil man in a long history of evil men.

Tobias was up. He moved like lightning. The squat man with the funny mustache was jerked back, yanked around, and pinned against Tobias's Hork-Bajir body.

Tobias's wrist blade was at his throat.

<NO!> I yelled.

The soldiers dropped cigarettes and canteens, swung around, and leveled their guns at Tobias.

<You know who this is? You know *what* he is?>

<No. And neither do you! Look at him. He's like some old corporal or something!>

<He's Hitler. He dies. End of story,> Tobias said grimly.

Hitler was frozen with fear. Trembling with a Hork-Bajir blade pressed against his jugular.

<Tobias, it's all different,> I said. <Visser Four changed it. All of it. No one is where they should be, doing what they did in our reality. We don't even know if these guys are the bad guys or the good guys in this reality.>

<He's still Hitler!> Tobias said.

<Is he? I don't know. Jake, in that other reality, the reality that comes from all this, was Jake still Jake? Was Marco still Marco?>

<You've got to be kidding! You're going to compare Jake to this walking piece of scum?>

<He's not evil for who he is, no one is. You can't be evil for *being* someone. It's what you *do*. And this guy's just a driver!>

From behind us, a new and sudden sound.

BOOM! BOOM!

The first tanks were firing down on the beach.

<Tobias, you can't do this,> I said. <You can't execute someone for what he might have done or even what he might do.>

"Release my driver, please," the German captain said tersely to Tobias.

Visser Four leaped, shackled hands outstretched for the Time Matrix. I bounded after him.

He took three steps. I took two. I clamped my jaws on his leg.

Pop! Pop! Pop!

The captain fired. Point blank at Tobias.

Tobias jerked in reflex. His wrist blade cut deep.

The driver — Hitler — fell to the ground.

Visser Four rolled with me on top of him. Rolled over, pulling me with him into a shallow ditch.

And overhead I saw the surreal vision of a bald eagle, six feet from wingtip to wingtip.

CHAPTER 39
Rachel

Ax and Marco were down. But not for long. They fluttered up out of the sand, fluffing their feathers, all damage repaired.

It was true. We could not be killed.

The same was not true of the soldiers. Two lay crying in pain. The others were silent.

I swooped down to land beside my friends. I suppose we must have looked like vultures arriving at the scene of death.

I closed my right talon around a grenade. I lifted it experimentally. It was heavy. Not as heavy as a salmon, though. I would be able to fly with it.

Marco and Ax each tried to lift one as well, but they were much smaller birds.

<One is all it will take,> I said. <Or at least one at a time.>

I grabbed the grenade firmly and began to fly. Taking off was hard, not impossible, but hard. I scooted across the bloody sand, flapped hard, turned into the breeze, and still barely became airborne.

But once I had wind beneath my wings, once I had clearance, I soared. The breeze lifted me up. Above the dead. Above the beach of slaughter. Out of line of the whizzing bullets. Too high for the shattering explosions of artillery.

Up I rose. Up and up, over the bluff.

The first tanks were lining up, depressing their main guns to fire downward.

<Forget them,> Marco advised. <We need to block the road. Keep the others from coming up.>

<Thank you, General,> I said, laughing. <I think I got it. Just need to pull the pin.>

<Not too early,> Marco pointed out. <How do we pull it?>

Ax said, <I can reverse direction. If I come back toward you and catch the pin in my talons, I believe the combined momentum will be sufficient to remove it.>

<Good plan,> I said. I turned into a tight circle, one wing low, the other high, tail spread wide to give me all the lift I could get.

Ax's harrier body flapped away, twenty, forty yards ahead of my flight path.

<This looks good,> I said.

<Rachel, how do you know how long that thing is fused for?> Marco demanded. <You could blow yourself up!>

<Hah-hah!> I laughed. <We're immortal, Marco. Jake was the death. We can't be killed!>

<That's not a bullet, it's a grenade. If it blows there won't be enough of you left to put back together!>

Ax turned back, flying straight for me. I flew straight for him. I held the grenade as low and far from my body as I could. I twisted it carefully, bringing the round ring out and forward.

<Just grab the ring, Ax. Just grab the magic ring.>

The distance closed with shocking speed. The harrier, the eagle, racing toward collision.

Closer . . . Closer . . .

Ax spun over on his back, reached, a sharp yank against my talons and a loud "Pop!" The grenade top dropped away.

I glanced back and saw the ring and pin hanging from Ax's talon. I looked ahead. A tank rolling past Cassie.

I had perhaps three seconds.

I was giddy. Filled with wild joy. I wanted to scream and laugh all at once. Maybe I did because as if from far off I heard Marco say, <She's crazy, Ax-man. Look at her. She loves this stuff.>

I looked toward my target. The hatch was open. The young, cocky soldier was shoulders up and out of the armored safety. He was turning a swivel machine gun toward the side of the road. Aiming at —

Only then did I realize that Tobias had grabbed a German soldier. That he was holding him and —

A sudden rush of movement. Visser Four, Cassie, an officer firing.

Pop! Pop! Pop!

Blood sprayed from the throat of Tobias's hostage.

The tankman's finger tightened on the trigger of the machine gun. I saw it all, every detail, every nuance of movement as though it were inches, not feet, away.

The hatch.

The trigger.

I released the grenade.

CHAPTER 40
Tobias

Bullets hit me in the face.

I staggered back. I felt my wrist blade cut. Cut deep.

A flash of movement overhead. I was still hawk in my mind and I knew that movement intimately well.

An eagle!

Flying low and slow, dropping . . .

FWUMP!

A muffled explosion.

The German officer jerked in surprise.

Then, the ammunition inside the tank caught fire.

Pop!Pop!Pop!Pop!

BOOOOM!

Flames shot from the tank hatch. Flames shot from the tank's gun barrel.

It stopped moving.

Flames erupted from the engine in the rear.

I climbed to my feet. A flash of Cassie with her jaws on Visser Four, holding him as he stretched futilely to reach the Time Matrix.

And then, a second explosion.

BOOOOM!

The tank's turret blew off. It twisted once in the air and landed.

It took a split second. Time enough for a wolf to react, to jerk back.

Not time enough for a human. Or a Yeerk.

The turret landed. It crushed Visser Four from the waist down.

The driver . . . the man who would, in another timeline, have been the most evil creature in human history, lay dead.

Soldiers lay dead or wounded, slammed by the explosions.

Rachel came circling down through the smoke. She landed on a dead tree branch. I expected her to be exultant. She wasn't. She said nothing.

Marco and Ax landed seconds behind Rachel. We were almost alone, the five of us. Alive, uninjured, surrounded by death and destruction of our own making.

The wounded moaned.

Cassie began to demorph. As soon as she had hands she went to the wounded soldiers. One French, one German.

"You'll be okay," she told the French soldier. "It's not bad." She ripped a few strips of the man's uniform, grabbed a stick, and made a tourniquet.

The other man, the German, died before she could even offer comfort.

"Humans?" Visser Four gasped, seeing Cassie. "Humans all the time?"

<That guy, that dead guy, the one with his throat all . . . he looks like . . .> Marco stammered.

<He is,> Cassie replied. <Or was. Or wasn't. I don't know.>

<These guys aren't wearing swastikas or anything,> Rachel said.

There was blood all over my arm. I began to demorph. It was the only way to remove the blood from my Hork-Bajir blades.

<It's all different,> I said. <It's D-Day, but it's not.>

<But these are the bad guys, right?> Rachel demanded. <I mean, these are the bad guys, right? Right?>

<I don't know, Rachel.>

<French and German allied? Hitler's some or-

dinary old soldier? This isn't the way it was,> Marco said. <This is messed up, man. The Germans conquered the French, and then the British and Americans invaded on D-Day.>

<There are no Americans,> I said. <There never was a United States. And Adolf Hitler was just an old man driving a jeep.>

<It is we who have now altered history,> Ax said. <In ways we cannot comprehend.>

I slipped out of my Hork-Bajir body. The blades gave way to feathers. The T-rex talons became my own smaller talons. I shrank and shrank and the bloodstains dripped away as they found less and less to cling to.

<The Time Matrix,> Ax said. <We have it now.> He was already halfway back to his own Andalite form.

My own hawk eyes returned, so superior to the Hork-Bajir vision. I turned my gaze on Visser Four. The head moved. He was still alive.

Then I saw a smaller movement. I fluttered my wings and hopped over. I darted my beak down and snapped up the gray slug that was crawling down the doomed man's cheek.

<The Yeerk,> I said.

The others came over. Cassie was human. Rachel mostly so. Marco as well. Just kids now, in a ditch, behind a burning tank, surrounded by bodies.

<What should I do with him?> I asked.

Marco held out his hand. He took the Yeerk. "We can't let him get a new host. Can't take him back to our own time. He knows now that we're humans. We leave him here, he dies slowly of Kandrona starvation."

"They say it's a horrible way to die," Cassie said.

Marco held the Yeerk out to Ax.

<No,> the Andalite said. <I have enough to answer for.> Ax looked at Rachel, then looked away.

"No," Rachel said as Marco offered the Yeerk to her.

<Not me, either,> I said.

"I see," Marco said, nodding slightly. "No one's anxious to add another stain on their conscience? Everyone's had enough?"

He flipped the Yeerk almost casually through the air. Threw it into the flaming hulk of the tank.

"Starve or burn," Marco said, trying in vain to sound tough and indifferent. "His only choices. This is quicker."

"We have to end this," Rachel said, sounding sad and sick.

"No. Not yet," Cassie said. "There's still the Time Matrix. And there's still Jake."

<How do we do it?> I wondered. <Go back to each place we went and . . .>

<We need to cut the chain of causality early,> Ax said. <If we can stop this Controller from finding the Time Matrix in the first instance . . .>

No one said anything. We stood listening to the massacre on the beach. The roar of tanks trying to force a path around the far side of the burned-out hulk.

Good guys or bad? Had we turned the battle for better or worse?

"My turn, I guess," Cassie said softly. "I guess none of us will get through this without some terrible sin. This will be mine."

<What are you going to do?> I asked her.

She walked over to the former Controller. Now just a human being. "What's your name? I . . . someone told us, but I've forgotten it. Who are you?"

CHAPTER 41
Cassie

"John," he gasped. "John Berryman. I'm . . . Is he dead? The Yeerk? Is he dead?"

"He won't bother you again," I said. I knelt down and wiped sweat from his forehead. It was running down into his eyes.

"You're humans," John Berryman said. "The Yeerks don't know."

I nodded. "We know. Yeah, we're humans. Mostly."

"Kids."

I nodded again.

"I'm going to die, here." It wasn't a question. I didn't deny it. He could not possibly survive the massive injuries.

"Mr. Berryman . . ."

"John. You kids. You're heroes, you know that? The Yeerks, they hate you so bad." He laughed. He coughed and choked up blood.

"Don't know how you did it," he rasped. "Following him through time. He was trying to change the world. Bitter, very bitter. Change time, make humans weaker, easier to conquer, then replace Visser Three. But it was too complicated for him. He didn't realize. Landed here. Expected Nazis. Told the Germans this was the main invasion, rushed the tanks forward. Only . . . different Germans. They arrested him. Too complicated, see?"

"It was too complicated for us, too."

"Wanted to kill Washington. Wanted to change Trafalgar. Kill Einstein. Push the allies back into the sea at D-Day. Other plans, too, but you made him rush. Panicked him."

<Why Agincourt?> Tobias asked.

John Berryman laughed. "That was for me. It was to shut me up. I never gave up, see. I fought him. All night I'd keep it up. Keep it up in his head."

"Keep what up?" Marco asked.

"Shakespeare. I played Exeter in the play. But I memorized all the lines."

I shook my head. "I don't get it."

"*Henry the Fifth.* I know it by heart. Shakespeare wrote a play about Henry at Agincourt.

Visser Four couldn't figure out how or when to intercept Shakespeare. Not enough definite data. So he was going to kill Henry to silence Shakespeare, to silence me."

"That's insane!"

Berryman nodded weakly. "Insane. That's what he used to feel: that I was driving him insane. Wouldn't give up.

"'We few, we happy few, we band of brothers;
For he today that sheds his blood with me
Shall be my brother; be he ne'er —'"

"Oh, God. I'm not going to be free. I'm dying. Oh, God."

"Mr. . . . John. I . . ."

He looked up at me, exhausted. Beyond anything but pain. "What is it? Ask me your question."

I wiped tears from my eyes. "John. I'm so sorry. But . . . John, do you know, did your parents ever tell you . . . How did they meet? When and where?"

I saw puzzlement. Confusion. Shock. And finally sad acceptance.

"San Francisco. 1967. My dad's name was John, too. My mom is Theresa. She was Theresa Knowlton."

I could feel my friends draw back from me.

Cassie, the killer with a conscience, the Drode had sneered. Kill 'em and then cry over them.

I wasn't going to kill John Berryman.

John Berryman would never exist.

CHAPTER 42
Ax

The Time Matrix was surprisingly simple to operate. It could be directed by thought-speak command. There were no codes to break, no subtleties to grapple with.

Cassie told me the time and place and date. I morphed to human, made physical contact with the Time Matrix, and my friends did as well, keeping their own minds blank as possible.

And then, very swiftly, we emerged in bright sunshine in the middle of a crowded street.

Two humans, one male and one female, were staring directly at us. They did not appear to be alarmed.

"Whoa! Cool," one said. He had a great deal of hair on his face and head. He wore colored beads around his neck. He wore vision augmentation devices with blue lenses. "Did you see that, man? I mean, is that like, *real*?"

The female had very long hair, also adorned with colored beads.

"What's real, man?" the female wondered. "Real is just like . . . it's like . . . you know, like whatever, right?"

"Right on."

"Love, man. Love is like . . . you know. Like reality, right?"

"Huh?" the male asked.

"Um, what?" the female asked.

The two of them nodded in unison.

"Amazing," Marco said. "The United States is gone, or at least way different; the Nazis never happened, Einstein, who knows? But hippies are right when and where they're supposed to be?"

"What are hippies?" I asked. "Hip. Pees."

"Dude, these are hippies," Marco said. "Look at this place!"

I did as instructed and looked around. There was a large number of humans with very long hair and colorful beads.

"The Drode said our own timelines were buffered, protected. Maybe the Time Matrix did that for John, too," Cassie suggested. "I mean, maybe while he was using it he couldn't disrupt his own timeline. This is part of his timeline."

Marco shrugged. "Or maybe hippies just had to happen, you know? Otherwise how would we have bell-bottoms?"

"Over there," Rachel said, nodding toward a store. "That's the place. John Berryman's parents, John Senior and Theresa Knowlton, will meet right there, today. All we have to do is separate them. They don't meet, they don't get together, they don't have a kid named John, and Visser Four ends up in some other host, in some other place. He never finds the Time Matrix. And none of it happens. Time isn't altered."

"We never travel back in time," Cassie said. "Jake doesn't die."

"Neither does a Hessian officer," I said.

"Or a tank full of soldiers."

"Or a Yeerk."

"Or Hitler," Tobias added. "How can we *do* this?"

"What do you mean?" Marco demanded.

"Oh, man, the colors, man!" A "hippie" had come up to admire the Time Matrix's shimmering globe.

"Right, the colors, whoa! Cool! Go away. We're trying to figure out the space-time continuum here," Marco snapped. "What are you getting at, Tobias?"

"Look, Visser Four changed history. Maybe for the worse. But maybe not. Hitler was just a lowly nobody. No Holocaust! We want to change it back so there *was* one?"

"You saw the way our future was," Cassie argued. "We still had slavery. We had no freedom. The Drode said homeless people were rounded up and shot. We can't let that happen!"

"But we *can* let the Holocaust happen?" Rachel demanded. "Tobias is right. That future we saw, that future we were in, that's back when Visser Four had done all he did, but without us getting in his face. That was the result *without* our intervention. Maybe in that timeline he did ten more things. We don't know what the result is *with* our intervention. Maybe the future is better now. Maybe us saving Henry, and even taking out that Hessian officer, I don't know! Maybe . . ."

"Heavy, man. Way heavy," a female hippie said.

"We could use the Time Matrix, travel back to our own time, see what's happened. See if things are good," Tobias said.

"Does that not seem foolish now that we see how complex that history is?"

"I'm just saying we go take a look," Tobias said. "See how it all played out."

"Hey, history is never 'played out,'" Marco said heatedly. "We start messing with the past, we mess with the future. Maybe we like the way things look to us back in our own time, but maybe we've screwed something else up down the line."

"We do that every day," Rachel said. "Every time we do anything, or do nothing, we change the future. Why is this different? Look, let's just go see. Maybe our own time is great now. I mean, maybe, right?"

"Why are we here?" a voice said.

CHAPTER 43
Cassie

Five heads snapped.

Six pairs of eyes stared.

Four mouths and one thought-speak voice said the same word.

"*Jake?*"

He looked annoyed. "Well, duh. Like you don't recognize me? Hey. How did we get back here?"

Here was my barn.

"You're alive," Rachel said to Jake.

He stared. "I really don't like the way you guys are looking at me. You're giving me the creeps."

<What happened?> Tobias wondered. <How the . . . oh, man. The hippie chick!>

"What? What hippie chick?" Jake demanded.

"It was Theresa Knowlton," I said. "We didn't have to make the decision. She saw us. She was distracted. She missed meeting Berryman's father. Berryman was never born. It all never happened."

"Excuse me!" Jake interrupted. "Why am I crossing the Delaware next to George Washington one minute and then I'm back here while you people babble about hippies?"

Berryman had never existed. The Time Matrix was where he'd found it. Buried.

We'd never gone back in history, except in our memories. Henry V had *not* seen a Hork-Bajir take to the field. Washington *had* crossed the Delaware and surprised the Hessian troops. Nelson and the British *had* defeated Napoleon's fleet. Einstein *had* left Nazi Germany to find freedom from oppression at Princeton University, where he had set in motion the creation of the atomic bomb.

And on June 6, 1944, soldiers of the United States, Britain, and France *had* begun the final destruction of the evil man who, in another reality, had been nothing but a harmless old soldier.

"You died, Jake," I said. "You died crossing the Delaware with Washington."

I could see the spasm of shock on Jake's face.

"Oh, my God," he whispered. "Did . . . I

mean, in the end, did we do it? Did we put it all back right? Did we make it right?"

I went to him and gave him a kiss on the cheek.

"No. We didn't make it right. But we put it back, Jake. Leave it at that. We put it all back."

Don't miss

#30 The Reunion

With a clean face and conditioned hair I headed toward the school bus stop.

And walked past it.

Instead, I hopped on a city bus headed downtown.

The warren of streets that is the financial and business center of our town seemed as good a place as any to kill time. To get lost without running the risk of running into anyone who knew me.

There were movie theaters downtown. I figured I'd look around till I could catch a matinee of something loud and fun.

Twenty minutes later the bus dropped me and thirty office-bound men and women in the heart of blue-suit central.

It was still way early but already the sun was heating up the sidewalks and the exhaust from the cars, trucks, and busses was spread like a grubby, smelly blanket over the concrete and steel jungle.

Nice choice, Marco. I should have gone to the beach. I stood on the sidewalk and stared.

Seething mass of humanity. I'd heard that phrase once and now I knew what it meant. It meant "office workers at rush hour."

What was the big hurry? Did adults really like going to work? Or was Friday free donut day at the office?

THWACK!

I was down! My knees hit the pavement and my face landed in a planter full of cigarette butts and abandoned coffee cups.

The enemy! I prepared myself for the next blow.

Nothing. I looked up.

No one had noticed I'd been knocked over.

I got to my feet, dazed. I rubbed the ash, dirt, and stale coffee off my face with the bottom of my shirt.

I was disgusted. And I was mad.

A woman had run me over with her tank of a briefcase. Then she'd continued on down the street like nothing had happened. And no one had stopped to help me.

"And they say my generation has no manners," I muttered.

I gave myself a quick once-over — nothing

seriously damaged but my dignity — and set out after the woman who'd so callously whacked me. This woman had an appointment with the dirty pavement, courtesy of a well-placed Saucony Cross Trainer.

I caught up to her about halfway down the block and followed a few feet behind. Waiting for my chance. Her briefcase was big enough to hold a Doberman and built to maim, with steel corners and a big combination lock on the side.

And what was up with that hair? The woman wore a stiff, curly blond wig. Think steel wool pad. Used. Slightly shredded. And yellow.

I saw the perfect spot to exact my revenge.

I skirted the crowd and hid behind a big, concrete column about a yard ahead, just at the corner of the courthouse. When Wig Lady passed — bingo, bango! BAM!

She was going down.

I peeked from around the pillar to see how close she was to meeting my foot. And then I bit my cheek to stop from screaming.

The woman with the awful blond hair and the briefcase . . .

Was my mother!

Visser One!